Web of Desire

Web of Desire

SOPHIE DANSON

First published in 1993 by
Black Lace
332 Ladbroke Grove
London W10 5AH

Copyright © Sophie Danson 1993

Typeset by CentraCet, Cambridge
Printed and bound by
Cox & Wyman Ltd, Reading, Berks

ISBN 0 352 32856 8

Black Lace novels are sexual fantasies. In real life,
always practise safe sex.

Chapter One

The early summer sunshine caressed Marcie's naked skin like a lover's fingertips, and she rolled over, catlike and luxurious, searching for Richard's animal warmth.

He grunted as her fingers playfully traced the long curve of his spine, her sharp little nails just brushing the tiny hairs on his golden-bronze skin.

'Wake up, Richard,' she breathed into the nape of his neck as she bent over and kissed it. 'Wake up and fuck with me.'

A little smile played over Richard's face, and the corners of his mouth twitched, betraying his wakefulness. Just as Marcie thought he was going to play dead forever, his eyelids flickered open, and his blue eyes blinked in the morning light. Rolling onto his back, he seized her arm and pulled her on top of him, crushing her against his burgeoning erection.

It felt good to be there on top of him, her thighs straddling his muscular body, her pubis crushed against the throbbing hardness that lay across his flat belly like a sleeping serpent. She would very soon waken it.

She began to rub her pubic bone against his erect penis, grinding with all her weight against his manhood, forcing him to acknowledge the strength of her desire.

'Little minx. I shall have to teach you a lesson.'

He reached behind her and, pulling up her flimsy silk nightdress, dealt her a hearty slap on her bare backside. With a little squeal she tried to wriggle out of his grasp, but he had her fast and was determined to make the most of the advantage. The flat of his hand rained blows on her naked buttocks, making the flesh sting and redden. But more than that: with the pain and indignity came a more insidious feeling, a creeping warmth that soon began to spread the most delicious sensations of pleasure into the heart of her intimacy.

Marcie's sex was warming, burning, almost aflame now with desire. Her clitoris had swollen to a hard bud, throbbing with an urgent need. All pain and anger forgotten, she gave up struggling and instead set about communicating her own desire to her husband. He was already panting with arousal, and each loud, driving, quivering slap he landed on her backside communicated more stimulation to his own straining cock.

To help him along Marcie slipped a hand between her body and his, and succeeded in grasping his hot hardness. He gasped at the sudden contact, and immediately stopped slapping her backside. Triumphant, she wriggled free of his grasp and slid down his body until she knelt between his thighs. She bent and took his cock into her mouth, sucking it into even greater hardness. He tasted salty, like some lively sea-creature, fresh from the ocean, and she imagined herself and Richard linked together in the cool water, far beneath the waves; never needing to breathe, only to kiss and suck and fuck.

She knew he would endure the delightful torments of her tongue for a little while, but he would not let her suck him to a climax. Richard was hungry now, hungry to be close, to be inside her. She let him prise her mouth off him, hoping that today he would be more adventurous than usual. Perhaps he would even repeat that wonderful drunken night of not so long ago, when he had flung her down on the living-room floor and eased apart her arse-cheeks, sinking deep into her like a knife into butter. She found herself dripping even now, at the memory of his delicious savagery.

But it was not to be. Richard ignored her backside, though she was sure he had reddened it quite alarmingly, and she winced as he rolled her over onto her back and spread her legs. Now that she had teased him in to wakefulness he wanted her, and he wanted her now. He didn't even take the time to pull her breasts from her nightdress, or excite her clitty with his fingers, as he did so well.

He parted her nether lips quite gently, and placed the tip of his prick against the entrance to her womanhood. With a single stroke, he was inside her. Marcie groaned, and thrust her hips upwards to take him deeper inside her. She scratched and clutched at his naked back with her fingernails, trying to excite him to some display of unbridled passion. She wanted him to take her like an animal, and as he slid in and out of her slipperiness she imagined herself as a forest creature being mounted by some snarling beast whose penis burned as it entered her, thrusting into her without the least pretence of gentleness.

She tried to spur him on with cries and powerful thrusts of her hips; but Richard, always and literally a gentleman, continued to make love to her gently, as though embarrassed by the passion her naked backside had inspired in him.

'Fuck me! Fuck me hard! Ride me, oh ride me!'

If he had wanted to punish her, he could not have done it more effectively. Marcie could not reach a climax, though her clitoris throbbed almost painfully for release. With a sigh, Richard spurted into her, kissed her and rolled back onto the bed, obviously quite unaware that he had failed to satisfy her.

Furious, Marcie grabbed his hand and placed it between her legs, forcing him to scoop up his own semen and rub it into her engorged clitoris.

'I'm sorry, darling. Didn't you come?' Realising his mistake, Richard set about masturbating her in the way he knew she liked: a finger working its way between her labia, and the flat of his thumb skating lightly over her clitoris. Gradually, Marcie sank into pleasure, forgiving him in spite of her anger.

Her orgasm washed over her in warm waves, and she sank onto the bed in release.

They lay together for a little while, drowsy in the early morning sunshine which flooded in through the half-open shutters. Richard was evidently quite contented, and lay with his arms

4

wrapped round Marcie, one hand cradling her breast.

But Marcie was troubled. She was still unsatisfied. She needed more – something more extreme, something beyond the realms of safe, pleasant, companionable sex. What was it: danger, pain, fear? She hardly knew. But her clitty was hard and throbbing once again, demanding attention.

When Richard got up to run a bath, Marcie pulled up the bedcovers and slid her hand under the sheet. Eyes closed, a half-smile about the corners of her mouth, she set about caressing the sinuous curves of her body.

She was an attractive woman, there was no doubt about that. Other women might have misgivings about their bodies, but not Marcie. She had spent her young life being pursued by men, and by one or two women, who were only too convinced of her desirability. It wasn't that she was conventionally beautiful – no, her abundance of red hair tumbled about a face whose lines were strong and vibrant, rather than classical. Her eyes were sea-green mirrors in which her lovers lost themselves, but which seldom betrayed the fluctuations of her own emotions.

As her fingers traced the fullness of her breasts, she fantasised about her perfect lover. It wasn't Richard, though Richard was good to her in his own way. On the whole, she was happy with him, though sometimes his amiable apathy made her so mad she wanted to hit him. Or was it really that she wanted him to strike her?

Her fingers slid silently down her belly and into the dense thicket of her pubic hair, toying with the strands, twisting them about her fingertips. She pulled at them, at first gently, then with greater force, enjoying the delicious pain that warmed her pubis and inflamed her swollen lips.

She let her left hand stray to her nipples, stroking and pinching one and then the other until she felt her insides flooding with warm desire. Then, with the fingers of her right hand, she parted the petals of her secret flower and let her index finger plunge in, like a diver parting the warm waves of some tropical lagoon.

Quickly, she sought out the pulsating bud of her clitoris. It yearned for her knowing touch, the touch that was the certain harbinger of delight. Only Marcie knew the secret passwords to the heights of her own pleasure, and she began to rub at her clitty – at first quite gently, then with greater energy, as she felt her pleasure begin, deep within her belly.

In her mind, she was being fucked by a man whose face she could not see. She was on her hands and knees on a cold, marble floor, and he was behind her. She could see no more of him than a dark shadow on the gleaming tiles. The coolness of the stone felt good against her warm flesh; but better still felt the burning of her backside, throbbing still from the cut and swish of his whip. She writhed in silent pleasure as he entered her from behind, quite roughly, paying no heed to her discomfort unless perhaps he intended to heighten it.

She dared not cry out, though he was shafting her with such force that her backside smarted and his penis rammed insistently against the neck of her womb. She dared not make a sound, for he would punish her severely for any transgression.

As her orgasm filled her, like a clear, sea-green liquid pouring into a crystal bottle, a little moan of pleasure escaped from Marcie's lips. She fell back onto the bed, sated at last.

She opened her eyes to see Richard standing in the doorway, his prick rearing skywards.

Silently he smiled, sliding under the sheets, the bath apparently forgotten, his tongue burrowing deep into her warm bounty, lapping up the fragrant juices of her joyful deceit.

Her sister's unruly kids had gone home after their week-long visit, so there was no-one to disturb their late, lascivious breakfast. But Richard had to go to work, as he often did at the weekend. Before long, Marcie was left to her own devices, with nothing more glamorous than the washing-up to look forward to.

She put on a dressing-gown, finished scrubbing the pots and then sprawled on the sofa for half an hour, watching children's television. She had meant to take a quick bath and then switch on the computer to check the money markets. But she felt lazy, imbued with sunshine and sex.

She must have dozed off, she realised as she woke with a start.

There had been noises; rustling noises.

Someone was in the house!

She scrambled off the sofa, pulling her robe around her, quickly deciding what to do. Picking up an iron doorstop for a weapon and for courage, she crept into the kitchen. She peered round the door.

Nothing. There was nobody there.

Then she felt the hands: touching her, tightening

about her shoulders, pulling her backwards. The robe fell open, its silky fabric parting, baring her nakedness, wafting the fragrance of her sex into the warm morning air. She opened her mouth to cry out, but no sound emerged.

The hands took hold of her by the waist, and turned her round.

'Hello, Marcie. Did I give you a shock?'

Marcie stared dumbstruck into Alex Donaldson's face. She didn't know whether to hit him or laugh.

'How the hell did you get in here? I never gave you a key.'

He grinned like a mischievous schoolboy, proud of himself.

'You left the window of the outhouse slightly ajar. It was easy to climb in. Piece of cake.' Noticing Marcie's expression of horror, he added, 'It's OK. Nobody saw me. Our little secret is safe.'

She wanted to shout at him, tell him if this was his idea of a joke, he could bloody well forget it. But he looked so abashed, almost boyish, as he stood there, his strong hands resting lightly on her hips, as though beseeching her to come to him, forgive him, make it all better.

His fingers moved from her waist and began exploring. Marcie looked down and saw how the robe had fallen away, slipping down her shoulders and exposing the firm rosebuds of her nipples, the red-gold triangle between her thighs. Transfixed, she watched as Alex's hands began to move over her waxy-white skin. It felt as though she were inside another woman's body, experiencing all her sensations. And she began to tremble with delight and desire.

Alex Donaldson was a good-looking man by

anyone's standards: a solid 35-year-old, all muscle, with a slender waist and broad shoulders. Fit and sexy, with naturally wavy golden hair and a close-cropped beard. Hardly what you'd expect in a financier who spent most of his day sitting behind a mahogany desk in the City. Marcie could have spent hours just tracing the smooth, firm curves of his muscles. But they seldom had the luxury of hours. Their relationship consisted of snatched moments of clandestine lust, wherever they could make excuses to be alone. It was easier for Marcie; working from home, at her computer terminal, all she had to do was to connect her answering machine and the world could go hang. But it was different for Alex: every moment of his day was planned in advance. Besides, they couldn't afford to be seen together. Not that Richard would be furious: he'd be very understanding about it, very civilised.

Too bloody civilised by half, thought Marcie, as Alex's strong fingers pulled and pinched at her hardening nipples.

Most of the time, sex with Alex was quickie sex: a raunchy fuck in a spare half-hour. But it was hot sex. The orgasms she had with Alex were much more intense than those she had with her husband – intensified, she was sure, by the spice of danger and the fear of discovery. With Alex, she'd enjoyed sex in hotel rooms, in store-cupboards, in bushes just a few feet away from a society garden party. Without him, her life would be pretty dull. And even with him, there seemed to be something missing.

But she wouldn't dwell on his shortcomings today. Far from it. As she looked down at his hands, she noticed a swelling at the crotch of his hand-sewn suit. Instinctively, she stretched out and touched it, letting its warmth soak into her hand. There was an electricity in his hardness, a pulsating life that made her wet with anticipation.

He nuzzled into her neck.

'You smell delicious, my darling.' He lavished kisses on her neck, her lips, her throat, her breasts. 'The smell of sex.'

She was still caressing his penis, sliding her fingers up and down the line of his zip, feeling his enjoyment swelling, hardening, pressing against the inside of his trousers. But when she made to take hold of the zipper and tug it downwards, he stopped her with a kiss, and to her surprise slid to his knees before her, pressing his face into her pubic curls.

Marcie began to moan softly as Alex's strong hands slid between her thighs, prising them apart, forcing her to slide her feet across the smooth, tiled floor. She felt dizzy, disorientated, as she gazed down at her lover, immaculately dressed in his dark business suit, his diamond cufflinks sparkling on the virginal white cuffs of his Jermyn Street shirt. He seemed so far away, cool, perfect, inhuman.

Almost like being screwed by a robot.

She wondered what it would be like to have a cold steel penis inside her, moving in and out of her soft wetness like some crazy piston. In, out; in, out; feel the steam building up, ready to blow; metal and flesh in unnatural harmony.

His face was pressed hard up against her inner lips, his tongue seeking out the centre of her intimacy. She could smell the strong scent of her

10

sex, the mingled animal odours of Richard's semen and her own sex-juice and sweat; and she knew that he could smell and taste the odours, too, and that they were exciting him to fever-pitch.

Her clitoris burned with a fever of expectation, a fire that could not be assuaged except by a man inside her. She tried to tell Alex, but the only sound that came out of her mouth was the moaning of a bitch on heat, the inarticula cry of all-consuming lust.

Alex looked up at her. His lips were wet and fragrant with her juices, mingled with Richard's semen. The sight of him, wearing the badge of her own lasciviousness, so excited Marcie that she at last found her voice.

'Fuck me, Alex. Fuck me, please, please.'

She was trembling like a little hind, waiting for a stag to mount her. She craved the rough rutting of beasts, the uncomplicated coupling of savages on the forest floor.

As though he had read her mind, Alex sprang to his feet and seized Marcie by the arm.

'You're hurting me. What are you doing?'

Without answering, Alex dragged her across the kitchen and through the back door, into the garden. Her silky dressing-gown slid from her shoulders and began to trail on the ground. She was utterly naked, utterly vulnerable in the unforgiving sun of an August morning.

Looking up into his face, she understood with a shiver what he intended.

'No, Alex. We can't! Not here.'

But Alex paid no attention. Instead he unfastened the belt which had held the dressing-gown about her waist. He pulled it off, quickly and efficiently,and threw it onto the warm grass under the apple trees.

Richard and Marcie had chosen the cottage because of its orchard: a dozen or more mature fruit trees, their gnarled boughs arching over the tufted lawns, touching in places to form a mottled green canopy. At the bottom of the garden was a stream, on the other side of which were more cottages, and the village shop. And there were also houses on other side: big, prosperous houses where respectable businessmen lived, put up shelves and had comfortable sex with their wives on Saturday nights. Even as she looked towards them, Marcie thought she saw the twitch of a curtain, an imperceptible movement behind the leaded lights.

She put her hands up to cover what remained of her modesty, but Alex was having none of it. He took hold of her wrists and pulled down her hands, exposing her bare breasts to the hot summer sun and to whatever eyes happened to be watching.

Marcie's head was spinning. She was unable to cope with the suddenness of Alex's unaccustomed initiative. The terror of being seen by her straight-laced neighbours made her tremble, but not just with fear. With a secret excitement. She thought of the Colonel and his wife; and old Mr Pearson, who'd most probably not had a woman for twenty years. What would he think if he looked out of his window right now? Would his flaccid old penis twitch into life? She suddenly liked to think of herself as a resurrectionist; liked to think of the old man gazing open-mouthed at her creamy breasts, the fine, smooth curve of her buttocks, the gingery triangle that marked the door to her sex. She imagined his trembling old hand fumbling with his fly-buttons, taking out his cock for the first time in years, and handling it with a half-forgotten skill.

And what about the Jameson-Laceys, over there in their big house? Marcie was pretty sure Andrea Jameson-Lacey hadn't had it in her for years. Her fat, middle-aged husband worked so many hours a day, he couldn't raise a smile. Well, Andrea, this one's for you, Marcie thought as she submitted graciously to her lover's incautious embraces, scarcely veiled by the overarching apple boughs.

He seemed intent on obliging her to display all her charms, bending and shaping her body into obscene postures. It seemed so strange to be naked, to be robbed of her every secret, while her demon lover stood before her fully clothed, directing the course of her humiliation like some Satanic ringmaster.

She was bending backwards now, knees bent and her supple spine arching until at last her hands met the softness of the grass and she was transformed into a shameless four-legged beast, its face upturned to heaven and its sex open to the eyes of the whole world.

The wind whispered through the apple trees, and the bees' drowsy hum spoke of secrets no longer hidden, of a soul whose deepest desire was also its most base. Marcie savoured her fall into decadence, welcomed it as she would welcome a new lover; she was beginning to realise that only a new excitement could cut through the weariness that was eating away at her, threatening to seal her forever within the tedium of a perfect existence.

But her guilty, half-realised dream was not to be fulfilled. Alex's mask of stern subjugation cracked into a grin, and he threw back his head and laughed. The spell was broken, the sweetness of degradation gone within the space of a single breath.

In a moment, Alex was upon her, rolling her onto her back on the soft grass as he tugged at the waistband of his trousers. And she was returning the passion of his caresses, at once elated by the novelty of the game and disappointed that it had not been taken to its uttermost extremes.

She felt for his cock. It was hot and smooth in her palm. She slid her fingers over the moist glans and down the silky-smooth shaft, lubricating it with its own slippery sex-fluid. The channel between her legs felt like a river of boiling desire, hot and wet and pulsating with its own secret rhythm. She ached for a finger on her clit, a shaft to stretch her sex, a hot rush of spunk to drown the fires of her lust. The air was full of the heady scent from inside her, the mingled fragrances of semen and desire. Marcie was dizzy with need.

'Fuck me, fuck me, now!'

With a single hard thrust, he slid into her, his eagerness grinding her soft white flesh into the sharp twigs and stones lying on the grass. The discomfort served only to excite Marcie more than ever. As his hardness penetrated her, she gasped and clutched at him, her nails digging into his back through the crisp white fabric of his shirt. Locked together, oblivious now to prying eyes, they rode together towards the summit of pleasure.

Marcie's orgasm was not long in coming; and

the convulsive spasms were enough to make Alex flood her with jet after jet of pearly semen.

As they lay on the grass, panting with satisfied desire, Marcie realised that there was a need still within her, a need not satisfied. The realisation filled her with apprehension, and with a strange excitement which she had never experienced before.

When Alex had gone, Marcie poured herself a glass of chilled wine and ran a bath. Just because her husband and her lover had abandoned her for the day, that didn't mean she couldn't pamper herself. She luxuriated in a sea of foam.

Afterwards, she scanned *Lloyd's List* and the *Financial Times*, then surrendered to duty and decided to do some work.

The computer was in the downstairs back room which Richard had coveted for a darkroom. But Marcie had immediately seen its potential as an office. In that dispute, as always, Marcie had come out on top. After all, if she was going to live in the back of beyond, and start running her freelance management consultancy from home, she was going to need a decent office. And that meant not being relegated to the kitchen or the box-room.

She sat down in front of the VDU, and switched on. She screen brightened and she booted up the disk, then tapped in the password, *JUNO*, and waited to access the network.

The money markets were quiet today. The US dollar was a couple of pfennigs up against the Deutschmark, but there was nothing that would alter the content of the report she was writing. She ran the graphics package and printed off a few bar-charts for the next board meeting. If she started on the report now, she could send it down the line to Head Office the next morning. You couldn't afford to be anything less than conscientious when you were freelance management consultant to the international conglomerate Grünwald & Baker.

She set up a file, but instead of looking at an empty page she found herself staring in disbelief as a message spelt itself slowly across the screen:

DON'T FOOL YOURSELF, MARCIE. YOUR SECRETS ARE ALSO OURS. WE KNOW EXACTLY WHAT YOU'VE BEEN DOING. OMEGA KNOWS EVERYTHING.

Chapter Two

Marcie's feeling of irritation persisted all day, and she woke up the next morning still wondering who had played that stupid practical joke on her. And why *Omega*, for pity's sake? What was it all supposed to mean?

But of course, there wouldn't be any significance to it, except to confirm that there were still a lot of people at Grünwald and Baker who resented her influence with the chairman. It was no secret that some of the young Turks, last year's Oxbridge graduates with their second-hand Porsches and immaculate girlfriends called Belinda, found her an irritation. A woman, still in her twenties and married at that: that wasn't the kind of person they wanted giving them orders.

Yes, there were a lot of people in Grünwald and Baker who had been unhappy when Stanhope-Miles decided to take on a management consultant to help put the company back on the tracks. And they certainly hadn't expected to get one like

Marcie MacLean. The fact that her consultancy was home-based annoyed them even more. After all, you can't run a proper professional business from your front room, can you? She had the feeling that they ranked the Maclean Consultancy pretty much in the same league as a sex-aids-and-Tupperware party.

Naturally, she was the first to admit that her lifestyle gave her a lot of freedom; but she detested the implication that she sat around drinking coffee all day, and the unspoken assumption that a pretty face goes hand in hand with a woolly brain. Mind you, their antipathy didn't stop them pinching her backside, or hanging around at the bottom of the stairs like smutty schoolboys to see if they could look up her skirt. The problem was that she was a highly-trained management accountant, not a fuffy-brained bimbo. She had MBAs coming out of her ears.

Undoubtedly they'd got wind of her dalliance with Alex, too. They might find that vaguely unprofessional. More likely they were just plain envious. But one thing was for sure: they'd prefer her as a secretary.

Well, today's meeting would prove that she had more than cotton-wool between her ears. The report she'd been working on showed quite clearly that Grünwald and Baker could improve its performance in the marketplace by up to ten per cent in the next accounting period, if they accepted the plan she had drawn up. There would be fireworks, but confrontation held few fears for Marcie. If anything, boardroom dramas turned her on. She'd often come straight home from a meeting and begged Richard to have sex with her, she was so hot for a good shafting.

She lifted Richard's arm from round her waist and slid out of bed, leaving him dozing, sprawled across the bed. He had a good, firm backside, she thought to herself, casting a wistful glance at his tanned flesh. Lying there, face down, thighs parted, he seemed to combine the innocence of a child with the sensuality of a gigolo sleeping off his latest excesses. His big balls were clearly visible between his parted thighs, golden-brown hair curling over the puckered pink flesh. And the twin fruits looked so tempting and juicy that Marcie longed to taste them. She thought of running her hand between those golden thighs and cupping the plump delights, taking them into her mouth, letting her tongue roll over the flesh, until it became taut with the expectation of ecstasy.

There was a glowing warmth in the base of her belly, and her nipples hardened pleasurably at her touch. She knew that if she slipped her hand between her legs, and just rubbed a little, there, between her parted love-lips, she could bring herself off, relieve the terrible tension. But there was no time to yield to her own desire. She glanced at the bedside clock: seven-fifteen already, and she still had the washing to do, the rubbish to put out and a note to write for the electrician. She decided to leave Richard where he was. It was his day off work today. Let him dream. She wondered who he was dreaming of.

With an effort of will, she turned her attention to the wardrobe, sliding open the door and scanning the rail with a critical eye. The blue suit? No, it was a bit too prim and proper. How about the

Armani special, the old standby? She took it out and held it against her, admiring herself in the mirror. It was classy, certainly, but was it too over-the-top? Today, she wanted to look her ravishing, sensual best, but with just a hint of menace.

Eventually she decided on the emerald green dress with the now-you-see-it-now-you-don't neckline. It had worked in the past, and there was no reason why it shouldn't work again. OK, she wanted to get by on her own merits, not on her cleavage. But she would use all the help she could get. She had a shrewd idea that tantalising glimpses of the unfettered breasts within the tailored bodice would be enough to lower their defences. If they were concentrating on her cleavage, maybe they'd be easier to persuade. Marcie had no silly scruples about fighting dirty. After all, nobody else did. Who knows? She might even get one or two clues to the identity of the practical joker behind the Omega message. Whoever he was, he was clever, even if he had access to the network. And he'd either found out her password, or he'd found a way to hack into her system without it.

And that thought, for all her self-confidence, sent a brief shiver of unease running down her spine.

She showered quickly, and dabbed a little dot of perfume between her breasts before stepping into the green dress. It was a good choice, showing off her long, shapely legs and firm bosom. Gossamer-thin stockings and elegant courts completed the look.

Richard was still asleep, arms round the pillow like a child with a teddy-bear. Clipping on her earrings, Marcie picked up her handbag and headed downstairs.

The journey to work was purgatory: the car was in the garage, having a new gearbox put in, so she had to take the train. Crowded into a stuffy carriage with hundreds of poker-faced people and their briefcases did nothing for the soul. What's more, the nagging throb of unsatisfied desire between her thighs threatened to ruin her powers of concentration. As she hung onto the luggage rack, sandwiched between tightly packed commuters, her backside rubbed tantalisingly against the man standing standing behind her. It was an involuntary movement, caused by the motion of the train, but with a guilty flush she realised she was enjoying it. Was she imagining it, or was he returning the favour, pressing his crotch against her backside? She could have sworn she felt a hardness beginning to swell inside his trousers.

He was pressed very close against her now, so close that she could hear his breathing. Was that his hand on her backside, caressing the contours of her buttocks, moving slowly downwards towards the hem of her short skirt? She realised that her own breathing was quickening, becoming slightly hoarse. An unknown man, whom she could not even see, was rubbing himself against her, running his disgusting hands over her flesh, in just about the most public place she could think of. And now he was pulling her skirt up, exposing her backside, bare save for a tiny pair of lace panties. Only the tightly packed crowds of commuters prevented her shame from being revealed to everyone. God only knew what he was going to try next.

And here she was, her nipples stiff and her clitoris yearning for him to go further, further, further.

Something touched her fingers. He had hold of her hand now. What was he trying to do? She could not pull free, even if she had wanted to, and her other hand was fully occupied in hanging onto the rail. She was at his mercy, and he must surely know it. His willing victim.

Her heart was pounding. She put up a token resistance, but felt her hand being pulled further back, until it made the inevitable contact. Instinctively, her fingers closed about the shaft of the man's naked penis, exploring it, sensing its excitement, its readiness. His fingers guided hers, showing her what he wanted her to do, but already she had guessed. He wanted her to masturbate him, this unseen man whose desire was throbbing in the palm of her hand, whose satisfaction was hers to grant or to deny.

Not daring to glance behind her for fear of what she might see, Marcie began to manipulate her unseen lover's penis, at first slowy and tentatively, then with greater energy. Part of her wanted to get it over with, to bring him off quickly so that he would go away and leave her alone. But a greater part of her longed to make it go on forever, to prolong the man's pleasure so that he would remember her, always, as the red-haired woman in the green suit who had one day taken possession of his soul. The understanding of her power brought with it a new excitement, and Marcie realised that she was so turned on by this unknown lover, this stranger wordlessly demanding the satisfaction of his intimate needs and desires, that she would joyfully have guided his engorged penis into the haven of her womanhood.

His shaft was already slippery with the clear love-juice trickling from his glans. Marcie's fingers slid up and down the hot, hard flesh as smoothly as if they were stroking satin. It all seemed so unreal, to be caressing the erect penis of an unknown traveller in the midst of scores of uninterested commuters some of whom were no more than inches away from her and who had not even begun to guess what was going on in their midst.

Marcie tried to picture the man whose cock she was pleasuring. She imagined his balls, tensing with the anticipation of release; his handsome shaft, thrusting like an arrow from his smart business trousers. But that was all she could imagine. Was he young or old? She had no way of knowing. This felt like a young man's penis, vigorous and hard. But what if she was wrong? What if she was handling some filthy old man, toothless and bald?

Even that thought did not diminish her excitement. In a way, the perversity of it heightened her pleasure. She felt wicked, depraved, liberated from the shackles of conventionality. Her body had become the servant, not of this man's pleasure, but of her own: the pleasure she was deriving from her power over the hot, hard flesh in her hand.

There was a shrill grating of brakes, and Marcie became aware of people trying to move about, struggling out of their seats and to take their briefcases out of the luggage racks. Waterloo already? The sight of arching girders overhead jolted her back to a different reality, in which she, a young financial executive on her way to an important meeting, was standing with her skirt hitched up over her backside, whilst rubbing the erect penis of a man whose face she had never seen.

The train lurched to a standstill at platform seven, and commuters spilled out of the carriage like grains of rice from a torn paper bag. Panic-stricken, Marcie tried to pull her hand away, while with the other she tugged her skirt down over her exposed flesh. Her unseen lover held her fast for a moment, resisting her with all his superior strength, showing her that perhaps she had been mistaken: perhaps she was not the one in control, after all.

Just when Marcie felt sure that she would be discovered, she felt the man's grip slacken, freeing her fingers. With a gasp of relief, she pulled her hand away from the man's penis. For what seemed an eternity, she stood stock still, not daring to move or to look behind her. Then a voice whispered in her ear, hoarse and with just a hint of menace.

'Until we meet again.'

And then his terrible, powerful presence was gone, leaving her white-faced and trembling.

'Excuse me, miss.'

She leapt out of the way to let an irritated businessman and a pregnant teenage girl push by, and watched them step out onto the platform. Was that him? Was the man in the blue jacket the one who had lured her into that dangerous, exciting game? No, it couldn't have been: his voice wasn't right. Marcie scanned the teeming hordes making their way down the platform towards the subway. There was no way of knowing which one of the grey-suited figures had been her fleeting partner in the packed railway carriage.

She picked up her briefcases and stepped out of the carriage, into the simmering heat of a summer morning. As she raised her hand to slam the door behind her, a heady scent wafted up from her palm. The scent of illicit, forbidden sex.

Jeremy Stanhope-Miles glanced up and gave a curt nod as Marcie entered the boardroom. She was amused to see that he was trying not to let his eyes linger too long on the deep furrow between her breasts.

Marcie took her seat at the table, her legs elegantly crossed to show just a hint of silky thigh. All eyes were on her, which was exactly how she had planned it.

She laid her two briefcases on the mirror-smooth mahogany, and took out overhead transparencies and laser-printed copies of her report, which she handed round the group. As each of the directors took a copy, she asked herself: is this Omega?

Not Stanhope-Miles, at any rate. The chairman was dry as dust, humourless; a career man who had little time for his wife Martha and four kids, let alone practical jokes. Probably not Peter James, either: he'd always been quite friendly towards her, especially after she'd helped him out of trouble on the Delhi project.

'Can I just run you through these figures?'

Marcie got up and walked across to the flip-chart. She took up a felt marker and started to draw, talk, persuade, seduce. She could tell they were against her, but on principle, not because of any logical disagreement with the facts. There was no logical argument against the facts. She believed in them implicity. And yet, there was doubt and resentment on their faces. Well, that was OK: she would use the facts against them. And if sex helped her argument along a little, so much the better.

As she spoke, arguing her case, drawing attention to the figures she had spent weeks drawing up, she looked around the room at her colleagues, searching for clues. Once she had worked out who it was, she could find out why. And plot her revenge.

Jayne Robertson, the Marketing Manager, was staring intently at her, as though trying to see into her soul. Marcie averted her eyes in discomfort. She knew Jayne had never liked her: she'd always resented Marcie's influence with Stanhope-Miles. It was just conceivable that she might have wanted to do something to hurt her. And yet Jayne didn't know the first thing about technology, and it was scarcely credible that she would resort to such a juvenile prank. No, Jayne Robertson would think of something more sophisticated and cruel.

Marcie switched on the overhead projector, and put on a transparency showing the projected savings from the cost-cutting measures she was suggesting. Mentally she was still running through the list of possible enemies. Harry Gates, Roland Palmer, Jon DaSilva: they were all possibilities. Young, ambitious men with a juvenile streak. Mary Dwyer, the chairman's middle-aged PA, might have been motivated by jealousy or simple moral disapproval, but it seemed unlikely. Marcie was left with the conviction that she was dealing with someone peripheral to the organisation, or even a complete outsider.

'These savings are based on no more than a two per cent fluctuation in the pound sterling,' DaSilva observed. 'What happens if there's a sudden run on the money market?'

'Yes,' Palmer nodded, with that horrible expression of smug self-satisfaction which had driven his girlfriend to pour lime-green paint over his new BMW. 'And these measures are all very well, but do you really think the workers on the shop floor are going to accept them? We'll have a strike on our hands.'

Marcie bent down, hands on the table, staring straight into Palmer's face. 'It's not a question of choice,' she said, very quietly and calmly, forgetting all her plans for verbal seduction. 'If these plans aren't implemented, the likelihood is that this company will go bust inside two years. Then nobody will have a job. And that includes you.'

There was a heavy silence while the words sank in. Marcie realised with a start that the glow of warmth had returned to her belly, her loins. There was something about power and aggression that really turned her on. In her mind's eye, she suddenly saw herself in black leather, grinding a spike-heeled boot into Roland Palmer's odious face.

'Of course,' Jayne remarked, 'we have only your word for it.'

'Indeed,' Marcie agreed coolly, refusing to rise to the bait. 'But if these plans aren't implemented, I shan't be staying around to watch this company sink. There are plenty of other employers, far more open to the idea of sound long-term financial planning.'

'Ah,' Palmer smiled. 'But would they all be willing to let you work from home, all cosy and snug? By the way, what's happening in *Neighbours* at the moment? Or does your work tire you out so much that you need a nice lie down?'

The implication was blatant, and it was lost on no-one. Marcie's sexual appetite was, if not legendary, at least common knowledge in the organisation. But she was classy, and she was more than choosy about her lovers. Those who had tried and failed to win her favours might understandably be resentful.

She smiled sweetly.

'Mr Palmer, you may spend your days screwing the company, but don't tar us all with the same brush.'

Her clitoris was pulsating with an insistent, throbbing beat; the beat of desire, as it surged through her body with every contraction of her heart. She wondered if the others could make out the hard points of her bare nipples, pressing stiffly against the bodice of her emerald green dress. The thought of them all staring at her breasts, witnessing her arousal, served only to excite her even more.

The rest of the meeting was less melodramatic. The board was more or less evenly split on Marcie's plans. They agreed the financial projections for the coming year; they could hardly deny the hard evidence. But the crunch came with the 350 planned redundancies. One thing was clear: this wasn't going to be sorted out in a single meeting.

'OK, I'm adjourning this meeting,' Stanhope-

Miles announced. 'Marcie, I'd like to thank you for preparing such a thorough breakdown of the figures. I, personally, have no doubt as to the necessity for radical measures, but clearly this needs further, balanced discussion to iron out the finer points.' He glared meaningfully at Palmer and DaSilva. 'And I don't intend to let personalities get in the way of making the right decision.'

Marcie gathered together her papers, on the whole well pleased with the way things had gone. She hadn't really expected to get her own way at the first attempt, and the level of opposition hadn't come as any surprise. In fact, all things considered, they had been quite reasonable. Of course, it had helped that she had an absolute, rock-solid confidence in the figures she had prepared. She had almost forgotten that she had dressed to impress.

She was no nearer to guessing the identity of Omega, though. Roland Palmer seemed just too obvious, somehow. His insinuations drew her suspicion as surely as a magnet. Or was it a double-bluff? Oh God, she was being silly now.

She had thought she was alone, but as she turned to leave, she noticed Harry Gates hovering by the window, as though waiting to ask her something. She walked past him, paying him no attention, and he caught up with her just as she was reaching for the door-handle.

'Marcie.'

'Yes?' She turned and looked at him quizzically.

'Would you like to go for a drink? Or a meal, maybe? I'm staying the night at the Portland Hotel, just round the corner. Do you have to hurry back home? I thought maybe we could spend a little time together, get to know each other better . . .'

29

'Sorry, Hal. Some other time, maybe.' She patted his hand, feeling more like his mother than a potential lover. He was quite sweet, really. Maybe . . . But no. Her love-life was complicated enough as it was; she didn't want to add any more random variables. 'Tell you what: why don't we have a lunchtime drink in The Feathers after the next meeting?'

Unsuccessfully concealing his disappointment, Harry disappeared along the corridor and down the stairs. He always took the stairs. He hated lifts, for some reason. He was obviously some kind of fitness freak, or severely phobic. Nobody walks down thirty floors just for fun.

Marcie turned right, walked towards the lift doors, pressed the button and waited. The lift was a long time in coming down from the fiftieth floor, and there was no one around. Surreptitiously, she undid the top button of her dress and slipped her hand inside, rejoicing at the touch of fingertips on nipple. It was hard, like a nubbin of warm steel, unyielding to the touch and yet so, so responsive. It felt as though she had electricity in her fingertips, crackling into her through her breasts, and surging along each vein, each nerve, until it reached belly and sex and arse and fingertips, completing a unique circuit.

A dull hum warned Marcie that the lift was on its way. She glanced at the indicator board. Floor 38: only a few to go. Regretfully, she slid out her hand and did up the top button. There was an uncomfortable sensation of dampness in her knickers. When she got home, Richard would get more than he'd bargained for. And if he didn't feel like it, well, she'd take care of that.

30

The lift arrived with a clanking of cables, and jarred to a halt at the thirtieth floor. The doors slid open, and Marcie saw that it was full. Obviously there'd been some sort of conference up in the penthouse suite, because everyone was wearing those silly plastic name-badges with the cardboard inserts. Without paying them much attention, Marcie stepped in and wedged herself behind the rapidly-closing doors. The throng parted obligingly to let her in, and she wriggled backwards into the midst of her fellow-passengers.

The cage jolted into life, and began slowly moving downwards. The journey seemed to take an age, as they stopped at every other floor for people to get on and off. The lift was unbelievably crowded now, and Marcie could hardly breathe. When she felt the hand on her backside, for a moment she thought it was an accident. Or was she just imagining it? In such a cramped space, it was inevitable that bodies would touch, you couldn't avoid it.

But no. There it was again. A slow, deliberate movement as the flat of a hand slid back and forth across her buttocks, exploring the territory, appreciating the firmness of the flesh tightly encased in crisp linen. Marcie's heart pounded, not for the first time that day. Was the world full of people with designs on her body? The thought made her shiver, not wholly with unease.

The hand was getting bolder now. Was it the same hand that had made its demands upon her in the crowded railway carriage, a few hours ago? Surely that was impossible. But she recognised something about the touch.

She tried to turn round, to get a glimpse of

31

whoever was doing this to her; but she was held fast by the tightly packed delegates. She could have asked one of them to help her, but something held her back. Maybe she should get out at the next floor? But the hand, sliding slowly, lewdly under her skirt, held her transfixed, as surely as if she had been chained to it.

The doors slid open at the fifteenth floor, and most of the delegates surged out of the lift, no doubt bound for the executive restaurant. Marcie took a step forward to follow them, but her wrists were suddenly held in a grip of iron. She made to wheel round in astonishment, intending to vent her anger on her assailant; but more hands were upon her, preventing her from moving, forcing her to stand still and stare forwards in despair as the doors began to close and her escape route was cut off.

Only fifteen floors to go. What could anyone do to her in such a short space of time? Although she could not see them, she knew there must still be five or six people in here with her, standing behind her and her captor. If she cried out, surely one of them would come to her rescue.

Between the fifteenth and fourteenth floors, the lift gave a little juddering movement, and suddenly ground to a halt with a loud grating noise. The lights flickered several times, and then went out. There was a terrible silence. The menacing gloom was broken only by the feeble glimmer of the emergency lamp.

No-one moved or spoke. The faceless presences behind her made no sound at all. Only their breathing reminded Marcie that she was not alone: their breathing, and the iron-hard fingers biting into her wrists and holding her neck in a vice-like grip. She must not panic. She must not show her fear.

And then she felt the brush of soft, silky fabric against the side of her face. She jerked her head away, but it was no use: the silk scarf was suddenly over her face, blotting out the last vestiges of light, the last comfort.

She was alone with the darkness now. Alone and blind, disorientated. Afraid. The hands were exploring her more boldly now, teasing her flesh, exciting her in spite of her terror. The lift was going nowhere. It could be minutes or hours before anyone got it started again. She was at the mercy of an unknown presence.

Skilful fingers were unfastening the buttons on her dress, easing down the zip, tugging the dress down over Marcie's hips. It fell to the floor with a gentle swish. Hands were still gripping her wrists, but she was no longer struggling. There was a strange, dreamlike inevitability about what was happening to her. The unreality of the hands pulling down her panties began to short-circuit the fear. A guilty warmth was spreading through her body, which was responding against her will to the symphony of caresses being played upon her buttocks, her thighs, her pubic curls.

'Obey,' breathed a voice close to her face, and she knew that it was the voice of the man on the train. 'Obey the discipline of pleasure, and you shall not be harmed.'

She wanted to cry out in anger, to protest that she was a woman, not a sex-doll; that she, Marcie MacLean, was not accustomed to submission; that she would not accept this would-be lover who

33

scorned her dignity and sought to impose his demands upon her. But she said nothing, for she was remembering that sultry afternoon, only the previous day, when Alex had dragged her into her own garden and stripped her bare with no regard for prying eyes. She was remembering the taste of his cock in her mouth, and the way he had thrust into her with sudden, unexpected mastery. She was remembering the pleasures of her own submission.

The hands were on her shoulders now, pressing her down, down, down. She sank silently to her knees on the floor of the cage. Blinded, she realised that her other senses had become sharper. The unmistakable scent of sex was all around her, filling the hot, stagnant air. The sound of a zip being pulled down sent a shiver running down her spine, and her nipples were stiff again, already anticipating what would be demanded of her next.

Fingers that were impregnated with the scent of her own cunt forced her lips apart, and the hand wound about her long, red hair brought her head forward suddenly, jerkily.

The man's penis tasted strong, salty. To her surprise, he did not try to ram it hard down her throat, like most men, half-choking her. He almost tantalised her with it, at first letting her have only the very tip of it, then gradually working his way in and out of her mouth. She ran her tongue over the glans with a dizzy fascination, picturing its purple head in her mind; picturing the heavy balls and the way the flesh tightened as his excitement increased.

With each movement of her lips and tongue and throat, she knew she was bringing him closer to ejaculation; and she waited with mounting pleasure for the flood of salty liquid that would fill her mouth with hot, white jets. Already she could hear his breathing growing hoarser, could smell his excitement, taste it on the tip of her tongue. She wanted to reach out and touch his balls, but the iron grip on her wrists would not let her go. Suddenly, she wondered who was holding her there. And how many others were there in the cage with her, watching, waiting, drinking it all in? She wondered if they were masturbating over her, if she was giving pleasure to them as well as to this faceless man with the large, smooth prick.

His cock was twitching on her tongue; soon, very soon, it would convulse with uncontrollable pleasure, and gush forth its tribute into her mouth. The sense of her own power was inescapable, and more erotic than she could ever have believed. She wanted to keep him there, on the edge, as he was keeping her on her knees before him. She wanted to toy with his pleasure, making him realise that he owed everything to her; and that, if she chose, she could deprive him of the satisfaction he so craved.

To her immense surprise, all of a sudden he withdrew from her. She felt instantly bereft, deprived of her one contact with reality. She understood at once what he meant by it: he was showing her that, whatever she might think, he was the one with power. He was her master, the only one in control of his pleasure.

Hands took hold of her and laid her down on the floor of the lift cage. The rough carpeting felt like a bed of nails against her delicate skin. She submitted to the hands obediently, passively; more

35

intrigued than frightened by what was happening to her.

The voice came again. It seemed far, far away; an echo from a different world.

'Pleasure yourself.'

For a moment, she did not quite grasp what was being demanded of her. Then her right hand was seized and guided to the red-gold triangle at the base of her flat belly. And she understood.

'Show me how you pleasure yourself. I want to see exactly what you do when there is no man to fuck you.'

'But . . . Why?' Marcie stammered. Instantly she knew it was a mistake.

'Silence.' The hand over her mouth smelt of cologne and leather and sweat and sex. 'No talking until I give you permission.'

Her fingers trembling with mingled emotions, Marcie parted the lips of her sex and ran her middle finger along the furrow, and into the dark warmth of her vagina. Already it was wet; after all, she had spent the whole day so far just barely below the threshold of overt arousal. Now a new stimulus had come to tease her clitoris into wakefulness.

'Touch your clitoris.'

'I – '

'Silence! Show me that you are worthy to speak. Spread your legs wider. I want to see your pleasure.'

Marcie's finger slid tremulously onto the hard bud between her labia. The scent of her own sex rose to fill her nostrils, adding to her shame, her excitement. She was aroused beyond belief now, and knew that it would not take long to bring herself to the apex of pleasure. The thought of the dark, faceless shapes in the lift cage, silently watching her in her nakedness, bringing herself off, only made her still more aroused.

And there was power, too, in her little demonstration. Power in the strong and skilful thumb of her right hand, pressing down with rhythmic regularity on her clitoris. Power in the fingers of her left hand, teasing and exciting her nipples. Power in the middle finger of her right hand, toying with the tight pleasure-palace of her arse. She knew what she must be doing to her faceless master, her cruel lover; knew, without needing to see his face, that his cock must be straining for release. And the very thought sent warm waves of pleasure surging through her belly. She was very near coming. Her cunt was dripping moisture. A few more strokes, just a few more, and she would be there.

'No!' The hand was on hers again, leather-gloved fingers gripping her wrist. 'You have not yet earned your pleasure.'

Earned her pleasure? The concept was an alien one to Marcia, for whom pleasure had always been as simple and accessible as picking chocolates from a box. The thought enraged and intrigued her. Who was this faceless man, to prevent her from having the orgasm she needed? And she so needed her pleasure, for her clitoris was throbbing with the almost unbearable pain of frustration.

She had no chance to protest, or ask him why. Rough hands were taking hold of her by the shoulders, turning her over onto her hands and knees, parting her thighs, exposing her naked buttocks.

He entered her with robotic precision; in utter silence, save for the sound of his breathing, staccato in the oppressive silence. In the sultry heat, she felt the sweat trickling down from her shoulders into the small of her back. The man's penis was thick; stretching the walls of her vagina as he thrust into her again and again. He made no attempt to pleasure her, pursuing his own satisfaction with rhythmic determination. It was like being fucked by a machine. Unreal. Mechanical. Without realising what she was doing, Marcie began to respond to the hypnotic beat, thrusting out her buttocks to receive the next stab of the well-greased piston. The coarse carpeting skinned her knees and palms, but she felt no pain. She was in another world.

He ejaculated into her without a sound, and withdrew quickly, leaving Marcie alone and unsatisfied on the floor. She tried to move, but the gloved hand was there again, on the nape of her neck.

'Do not move. I forbid it.' The scent of fine leather, mingled with the scent of sex, filled the stiflingly hot atmosphere.

All at once, the lift groaned into life, and through the flimsy fabric of the silk scarf Marcie saw the lights flicker back on. They travelled one, perhaps two floors, and then the lift stopped again. She heard someone pressing the button, and the doors slid open. Footsteps passed by: they were leaving! They couldn't leave her like this!

As he stepped out of the lift, the faceless lover turned and spoke once more. His voice was heavy with sarcasm.

'Until we meet again.'

And he was gone, the lift doors sliding shut behind him.

Left alone in the lift, Marcia realised that she must act quickly. Luckily, the lift had stopped moving, but she had to dress herself before someone called the lift and saw the state she was in. She tipped the scarf from her eyes and pressed her face against the little glass window in the lift door, blinking in the unaccustomed light. There was no-one in the corridor outside.

Hurriedly, she slipped on her dress and shoes, using the cast-off panties to clean herself as best she could. The evidence of her bizarre ordeal was everywhere: the whole lift reeked of sex, and there were little white stains on the carpeted floor.

When at last she was ready, she took a deep breath and pressed the button for the ground floor.

What was happening to her life? She picked up the black silk scarf and felt a surge of guilty excitement, knowing in her heart of hearts that her life was irrevocably changed.

Chapter Three

When she got home she found Richard in the garden, sprawled on a sunbed and holding a can of cold beer. He looked up and smiled.

'Care to join me?' He wriggled across the sunbed, making room for her to lie next to him.

'Why not? But I need a shower first.'

Marcie had already showered in the washroom at the office, but her clothes and skin were still permeated with the indelible scent of guilty pleasure. It was strange. She had never felt guilty about pleasure before: after all, wasn't it her right? But there had been something unique about her excitement as she lay on the floor of the lift cage, pleasuring herself shamelessly for the benefit of God knows how many unknown men. She wanted to wash it all away and forget about it; and yet, she also wanted it to linger and grow and take her over, guiding her, blindfold, towards heights of pleasure she had never imagined.

She undressed and threw her clothes into the

washing machine, then went upstairs and turned on the shower. The icy-cold water hit her skin like a thousand tiny needles, and she gasped with the shock of it. But it was wonderful to wash away the day, the heat, her cares, the stresses of the meeting; to soap her tired skin and feel it awake, refreshed and once again ready for excitement.

Her hand passed between her thighs, and a dull throb of desire reminded her that she had still not come off today. Her nipples were rock hard, not only because of the cold. Turning up the warmth a little, she relaxed under the tepid waterfall, and parted her thighs to allow her fingers inside her intimacy. She ran the bar of soap lasciviously between her pussy-lips, and the perfume mingled with her own scent, heavy and unmistakable. The creamy lather soothed and excited, helping her fingers to slide subtly over the sensitive flesh, skirting the head of her clitoris, which was too sensitive by far to be touched directly. Lukewarm water trickled down her belly and ran between her legs, exciting her with the gentlest of caresses. If she did not come this time, she would surely die of frustrated desire.

As she masturbated with the soap bar, her mind filled with pictures of the sunlit orchard, of fucking gently on sweet soft grass with the sun high up above, warming a red glow through her closed eyelids. But as she rose towards her climax, clenching her thighs together in an unvoluntary spasm of passion, a shadow appeared at the corner of her vision, masking the sun's rays, as though forcing her to open her eyes and acknowledge its presence. A dark shadow: a faceless figure, nameless and menacing. She knew that if she opened her

42

eyes she would see it: the long, smooth, hard cock emerging from the dark clothes, threatening her with its desires.

There was a voice, too; dark and husky:

'Want you, want you . . .'

And a hand gripped her as she came to a massive, juddering orgasm, at last finding refuge in the pleasure that had eluded her all day.

As the last waves of her climax ebbed away, Marcie opened her eyes to find that the hand belonged to none other than Richard, now completely naked and clearly moved by what he had seen.

'I want you, Marcie.'

Silently, he climbed into the shower beside her. His dick was big and beautiful, and Marcie wanted to take it into her mouth; but Richard had other plans. Grabbing hold of her hips, he hoisted her up effortlessly until her legs were round his waist. With no more difficulty than if she had been a doll, he lowered her gently onto his penis. She clung onto him, clawing at his back with renewed passion as he entered her. He controlled the movements, refusing to let her get carried away and come too soon.

He made her lean back a little, so that he could take her nipple into his mouth. Marcie loved it when he sucked at her, like some grotesque baby greedy for its mother's sex. She almost came as he gently teased the erect flesh with his tongue and teeth, and continued thrusting, thrusting, thrusting into her in almost unbearably slow motion.

'I'm coming!' she gasped, as she felt the pleasure building up at the base of her belly, spreading to her thighs, her buttocks, her breasts; and at last exploding in a crescendo of fragrant liquid.

Richard's semen shot into her so forcefully that she felt the hot liquid spurting against the neck of her womb. It was a dizzying experience, and she fell forward onto his shoulder, a helpless rag doll of spent sensations.

Later that evening, she opened the door to her office and went in to get some papers. Damn: she'd left the computer switched on. She really shouldn't have done that – someone might gain access to confidential information.

She crossed the room to switch off the machine. As she pressed *EXIT*, the machine flashed:

MESSAGE IN MAILBOX

She entered her password, and called up the electronic mailbox. Just one message for her. She read it with an unmistakable frisson.

DID YOU ENJOY YOURSELF IN THE LIFT, MARCIE? THUS FAR, OMEGA IS PLEASED WITH YOU. WOULD YOU LIKE TO DO IT AGAIN?

'My God, Marcie! Do you need a hand?'

Sonja Graham put her head round the door of Broom Cottage and surveyed the scene of devastation. The tiled floor was under a good inch of soapy water.

'The bloody washer's on the blink again.' Marcie, barefoot and in shorts, was fighting a losing battle against the flood, trying unsuccessfully to sweep the water out of the open door. The water level was still rising.

'It would help if you turned off the machine.' Sonja took off her shoes and waded across the

44

kitchen with her skirts hitched up. 'If you're not careful, you're going to electrocute yourself one of these days.' She switched the washing machine off at the mains and turned off the water at the stop cock. The machine gave up with a clatter, and stopped pumping out water.

Marcie and Sonja looked at each other across the receding waters, and burst out laughing.

'Tell you what,' Sonja said, picking up a mop and bucket. 'We'll clear this up, and then I'll take you into town for lunch.'

Marcie took a long drink of cold mineral water, and sank back into the wicker chair.

'This is a wonderful place. I love coming here. Thanks for suggesting it. You know, there are days when I forget I'm supposed to be an aspiring captain of industry, and start thinking I'm Mrs Mopp.'

Marcie speared a slice of avocado and savoured the buttery taste as it melted on her tongue. She looked up to find Sonja gazing at her with a little secret smile.

'How's Alex, then?'

Marcie grinned.

'Shh. You're not supposed to know, remember?'

'Oh come on, Marcie. You know I'd never say a word to anybody. You were great when Jim and I were going through our bad patch. Do you remember the time you decided to cheer me up, and took me to that all-male strip show?'

'How could I forget? I mean, you got off with the star of the show.'

Sonja giggled.

'You could hardly blame me, I was obscenely

drunk. Do you remember? And there was this huge, hunky guy with biceps like melons, inviting me to stroke his dick through this tiny little red g-string! What red-blooded female could resist an offer like that?'

'What happened after he invited you to his dressing room? You never did tell me, you know. Whenever I asked you, you always simpered and winked at me.'

Sonja washed down avocado with a swig of white wine.

'Well, seeing as it's you. And besides, I'm sure you've already put two and two together. Rick – that was his name – met me at the stage door and asked me into his dressing room. I was a bit taken aback when I got in there, I can tell you, because he was sharing with two other guys! I very nearly turned and ran back out again!

'Anyow, Rick saw I was worried and asked me to sit down and make myself comfortable. He was really sweet. I mean, he gave me a drink, and talked to me and in the end I did start to feel more comfortable with him. I think the drink had a lot to do with it. I'd never have dared stay in a room with three half-naked strangers if I wasn't already three parts pissed.

'I thought Rick's two friends, Andy and Jed, would get dressed and leave; but instead, they sat down and started chatting to me, too. They paid me all sorts of compliments about my hair and my clothes, and Jed leant over and sort of stroked my right breast. He was supposedly just feeling the fabric of my dress, but he and I both knew there was more to it than that. At any rate, my feelings soon became perfectly clear, because my nipples

46

stood straight up, all hard and shameless. I wasn't wearing a bra, because it was a backless dress, and so of course it was perfectly plain that I was open to persuasion.

'I was being quite calm and collected, or so I thought; but when Rick stood in front of me and unfastened his g-string, I thought I was going to go stark, staring mad. He untied the little bows that held it on at the sides, and then just left it there, barely concealing his greatest showbiz assets. Then he took hold of my right hand, as gently as can be, and showed me what he wanted me to do.'

Marcie leant across the table, her face alive with interest.

'So what *did* he want you to do?'

'He wanted me to take off his g-string. And I did! And he had the most wonderful dick I've ever seen, bar none.'

'Better than Jim's?'

'Oh, a good inch and a half longer, and I don't know how much thicker. It was still floppy, but even so it was almost as big as Jim's is when he's got a hard-on. Anyow, it didn't stay floppy for long, because Rick said "would you like to see a little party trick of mine?" So like a fool, I said yes. And do you know what? That man can get a full erection in under ten seconds, just by thinking about it!

'Well, by now I was all giggly and silly; but I knew what I wanted and the drink had broken down all my inhibitions. When Jed and Andy peeled off their g-strings too, I got hot and wet between my legs. Marcie, I was so hot for it, I'd have done it with anyone – and the thought of doing it with these three hot and horny guys was enough to turn me to jelly.

'Rick didn't bother getting me to take off my dress. He just knelt down, in between my thighs, and slid his hands up underneath my skirt. I wasn't wearing any stockings, and he didn't bother taking my panties off. He just pulled the gusset to one side, and then went down on me. Marcie, it was amazing! I get wet even now, when I think about it. He had a long tongue, and knew exactly what to do with it. He started off by running his tongue along the outside of my pussy-lips, and that was fantastic; but when he actually starting lapping at my clitty, well I couldn't last out long. After a few moments, I was climaxing in his mouth and moaning for him to do it again.

'By then, I was past caring about anyone finding out what I was up to, and I knew with these guys, I could just keep on having orgasm after orgasm, they were so skilful. So when Rick pulled me to my feet and asked me to sit down on his cock, I was only too happy to oblige. He slid into me like a hot knife into butter, and I felt his heavy balls slapping against my backside. He hitched my skirt up round my waist and made me spread my legs wide, so I could see myself in the mirror opposite. And, of course, so Jed and Alan could get the full benefit, too. By now, they were stiff and ready, and I guessed I featured in their plans.

'Watching myself getting it from a complete stranger was one of the weirdest things I've ever done, and one of the most exciting. It was like watching a dirty movie and being in it too, all at the same time. I could see Rick's shaft moving in and out of me, and I could feel it too – it was ramrod-stiff and so well lubricated that it slid in and out without pain, even though it was so large. He reached around in front of me, and I watched mesmerised as his finger found my clitoris and began to rub it.

'I cried out as I came, and my orgasm was all the more intense because I could see my pleasure in the mirror in front of me. And when Rick spurted into me, I saw the spunk oozing out and trickling down onto the chair cushion.

'Perhaps I thought that would be the end of it: a quick screw, and I'd get dressed and get out. But I'd reckoned without Alan and Jed, who had been gently stroking their cocks as they watched me with their friend. I think they knew that I wanted to go on fucking all night, and they were only too ready to oblige.

'Before I'd really recovered from Rick's screwing, I felt strong arms around me, lifting me to my feet. With a swift, skilful movement Alan pulled down the zip on my dress, and eased it down over my hips, letting it fall in a little heap around my feet. Rick's spunk was trickling down my thighs now, and you can imagine how I felt when Jed knelt down in front of me and started licking it off my skin! He licked it all off, right up to my cunt, and then ran his tongue round my labia – just like a cat lapping up cream! The sensations were out of this world.

'When he'd finished, he and Alan pulled me down onto the floor and laid me down on my side. I thought that one of them was going to screw me, but it turned out to be both! Jed got down on the floor in front of me, and slid his big prick into me. It slid in just like silk. Then I felt Alan lie down behind me, and start gently prising apart my bottom-cheeks. Oh Marcie, I was so scared. No-one had ever had me like that before! I was scared he would hurt me, but he must have smeared some sort of cream over his cock, because he slid right into my bottom with no pain at all. It felt wonderful.

'So there I was, sandwiched between two of my lovers while the third looked on and rubbed his cock back into stiffness. The sensations in my front and backside were incredible. I thought I was going to die! And I came again and again, before at last my lovers shot their loads into me and we lay there in an untidy heap, just giggling with the sheer pleasure of it all.'

Marcie took a bite of chicken.

'It sounds amazing. Was that the end of it?'

Sonja laughed.

'Oh, far from it! As soon as we'd all recovered, it started all over again. I don't think I've ever been fucked so much in an entire week, let alone in one evening! And of course, Alan and Rick and Jed were supremely fit, being body-builders and strippers. Their stamina was incredible. They could keep going, again and again. I spent the whole night in that dressing room, and I learned things I'd never dreamed of before, let alone tried.

'I left the next morning, and told Jim I'd spent the night with a girlfriend, talking over our problems. You know, that night changed an awful lot of things for me. I'd never really thought I was desirable, and certainly not a sexual adventuress. But after that night, I suddenly saw that sex didn't have to mean me lying on my back, waiting for Jim to hurry up and get on with it. I don't think

Jim could understand what had happened to me. I threw myself at him, and we spent the whole of the next day in bed. Jim nearly got the sack!'

Sonja paused for breath. Her cheeks were glowing with excitement, and her eyes were bright with the memory of her one, beautiful adventure.

'How about you, Marcie? What have you been up to since I last saw you? You must find my one night of lust pretty boring.'

'Oh, my life's not so very exciting, you know,' Marcie protested. 'Richard's hardly ever there, what with this new project they're working on at the Ministry; and Alex is fun, but . . . sometimes I want more.'

Sonja's eyes widened.

'Marcie! You've got a sexy husband with an adorably big dick, and a lover who dotes on you and is endowed like a stallion. You could have sex twenty-four hours a day if you wanted to, and what's more you've got a great job and a wardrobe full of clothes. What on earth is the matter with your life? It sounds perfect to me! Fancy doing a swap? You can have Jim and my boring office job, and I'll have Richard and Alex and the key to the executive washroom.'

Marcie laughed, suitably chastened.

'You certainly know how to put me in my place.' She placed her hand on top of Sonja's, suddenly anxious for the assurance of closeness. 'It's not that I'm unhappy with my life. In many ways, it's perfect. Perhaps it's a bit too perfect. I don't really understand it.

'But Sonja, just lately some very odd things have been happening, and I'm scared. Really scared. I've been given glimpses of a world that I don't want to know about. It's dark and it's terrifying. And do you know what, Sonja? It excites me.'

'I don't understand. What are you talking about?'

'I'm not sure yet. But some pretty freaky things have happened to me in the last few days. I've played with a man in a crowded train carriage, without even seeing his face, for God's sake! Imagine what would have happened if I'd been caught. I've been blindfolded and screwed in a lift by the same man, I'm sure it was. And I still don't know who the hell he is, or why he picked on me.'

Sonja stared at her, clearly perplexed.

'It all sounds a bit far-fetched, Marcie, even for you. Are you sure it isn't all some elaborate practical joke?'

'If it is, Sonja, it's a *very* elaborate one. For one thing, there are the messages.'

'Messages? How do you mean?'

'On my computer screen. I keep coming home and finding these cryptic messages in my electronic mailbox. Some of them are creepy; some are suggestive. Some are downright obscene. And they're all supposedly from some guy called Omega.'

'Maybe Richard is leaving the messages on your computer, to spice up your sex life a bit.'

'Maybe.' Marcia looked doubtful. 'But Sonja, Richard doesn't know how to use my computer. He's hopeless with technology, you know that. Yes, OK, he could learn, but he'd never be able to find out my password, surely. It's strictly confidential, and I've never divulged it to anyone, not even him. There'd never be any reason to tell him anything like that. I even confronted him with the latest message, and he looked genuinely baffled. I can only think it's some bastard at G and B, who wants to scare me or something.'

'Could be some guy who fancies you, and is annoyed because you haven't come across. Or maybe someone who's jealous of your success. What about that nasty little wanker who tried to lay the blame on you for the drop in share prices last year?'

Marcie sighed.

'Maybe. But it does scare me. And sometimes . . .'

'Yes?'

'Sometimes it arouses me.'

She could see that Sonja was both shocked and intrigued. Should she tell her what had happened to her, that day in the lift cage? Should she tell her that, only three days later, a man had slipped a strange silver object into her hand? She put her hand into her pocket and withdrew the object, laying it on the table in front of Sonja. It was small, about an inch long, formed like a crocodile clip.

Sonja gazed at it in puzzlement.

'A silver clip? What's it for?'

Marcie glanced round. They were in a dark corner of the restaurant: no-one would notice. She unfastened her two top buttons, and exposed one rose-tipped breast. The jaws of the silver clip fastened tightly, greedily on the tender flesh, sending a burning, darting, sharp and exquisite pain through her body. She gave an involuntary gasp.

Sonja was staring at her in amazement.

'Doesn't it hurt?'

'Pleasure and pain are incredibly close together.' Marcie's voice was soft and distant, as though her

53

mind was absorbed with the sensations. 'That's something I'm only just beginning to learn.'

Dragging herself back to reality, Marcie loosened the jaws of the clip, placed it back on the table, and fastened her blouse. Sonja picked up the clip and held it up to the light.

'There's something engraved on it. A symbol of some sort. I think I vaguely recognise it.'

'It's a Greek letter O,' Marcie explained, all semblance of a smile draining from her face.

'I don't understand.'

'Omega.'

That night, Marcie finished work late and slid quietly into bed beside Richard, thinking that he was asleep. She lay there for a few moments, just listening to him breathing, rhythmic and soothing in the darkness. Surely nothing could harm her. Surely the whole elaborate scenario was nothing more than that: a skilfully-crafted nightmare, designed first to frighten and then to lure her. Yes, that was it. Someone who resented her was trying to get her to expose her sexual weaknesses, and thereby humiliate her. Perhaps even now they were gathering evidence against her.

Her stomach tightened as she thought of herself, naked and willing in the lift cage, the power of her lust dripping from her oozing sex, glistening on her parted thighs. Her sexuality had always been a simple thing, an appetite to be satisfied. But now it was becoming complex and disturbing. She could feel it gaining a strength of its own, refusing to be restrained by obligation or inhibition. She was afraid of its power, afraid that one day she would let her mask slip in some terrible, irrevocable way.

Instinctively, she drew closer to Richard and pressed her nakedness against his back. The night was hot, oppressive; and his flesh was sticky with a light film of sweat. The animal odour of him was reassuring. She stroked his back and buttocks very lightly, like the breath of a breeze.

Richard stirred and rolled over, capturing her with his eager arms. His hardness pressed against her belly, demanding entrance.

'Want to fuck, darling?'

He slid down her body, worshipping her with tongue and lips; brushing the crests of her nipples, tracing a path of kisses between her breasts, down the soft curve of her waist. He ran his tongue down her belly and into the fiery forest of her pubic hair, teasing the curls and venturing almost, but not quite, into the pleasure-centre of her womanhood.

Marcie began to moan softly, twisting and turning under this delicious torment. Her hands clutched instinctively at Richard's shoulders, at his golden-brown hair, at his face. She wanted to feel his tongue on her clitoris, feel the incredible warmth in her belly turn to fire as the first spasms of her orgasm racked her body.

'Lick me! Oh Richard, please, please!'

He lingered for what seemed an eternity on the threshold of her desire, then gently took hold of her love-lips and pulled them open, exposing the throbbing heart of her sex. Marcie spread her thighs, drawing her knees up, begging him to enter her and release her from her torment.

But his tongue was coy and skilful, teasing

without satisfying. He ran its tip around the inside of her outer labia, writing a symphony of sensations on her hungry flesh. The clear sex-fluid was running freely from her womanhood, fragrant and sweet; a honey-dew of love that he lapped up as readily as if he were a humming-bird sipping nectar.

Then he began to tease the inner labia, and to brush the flesh around her clitoris with the merest whisper of a touch. It was unbelievable what Marcie could be made to feel, just with that tiny amount of contact. She began to touch herself, hoping that she could defy him and bring herself off by pinching her own nipples. But he was resolute, and his skill was too great for her. Her head was swimming with thwarted desire. She imagined herself floating forever in this terrible, wonderful limbo of near-orgasm. If only he could take her to the peak of orgasm and hold her there, suspended in ecstasy, for eternity.

His tongue still refused her clitoris any direct contact. She tried to force his head deeper between her thighs, tried to persuade and cajole him to lick her off properly; but he obviously intended to tease her for a long time.

And then a thought came into her head; a wicked, lascivious thought that fascinated her, as the fox's eyes fascinate its terrified prey.

The clip. The silver clip.

Stretching out a hand for the bedside table, she slid open the drawer and took out the clip. It felt cold in the hot palm of her hand. Its jaws were cruel and unfeeling. They would show her no mercy.

It was dark. Richard would not see. And if he

did, he would not care. He would assume it was just another of her little fancies and fantasies. She forced open the jaws of the clip, and with a trembling hand slipped them over her right nipple, which was already engorged. She let the jaws snap shut.

The pain seared through her with a burning intensity, and Marcie's back arched in agony. An agony which quickly faded, and was replaced by a sensation which was equally intense, and yet was compounded of the purest pleasure. The burning became a soothing warmth, spreading through her entire body, awakening every nerve, quickening her pulse, sending the blood rushing through her veins. And a picture came into her mind.

The picture of a hand, tightly gloved in black leather. A hand squeezing the silver clip tighter and tighter. A hand squeezing the pleasure out of her as surely as it inflicted the pain.

With a faint cry that was beyond both pleasure and pain, Marcie rached out and welcomed the orgasm as it crashed down upon her, powerful spasms tensing her cunt again and again. The image of the gloved hand did not fade until the last wave of pleasure had receded, leaving her spent and trembling.

Thwarted, Richard thrust his cock into her, determined to exact more orgasms from her. He forced his kiss upon her lips, and she tasted the juices of her own delight as he rode her like a man possessed.

Afterwards, they lay entwined on the crumpled sheets. Richard was dozing, and Marcie took the opportunity to remove the clip surreptitiously, and place it gently on the bedside table.

He stirred a little, and opened his eyes, a glimmer of moonlight giving them an unearthly gleam.

'Richard.'

'Yes?'

'What does Omega mean?'

'It's the last letter of the Greek alphabet; but mostly, people use it figuratively. You know: Alpha and Omega, beginning and end. Literally the last word, if you like. Why? You're not fussing about those damn stupid messages again, are you?'

Marcie reassured him that she wasn't, and rolled over, ostensibly to go to sleep. But she was reading the computer screen over and over again in her mind.

Alpha and Omega. Omega, the final, the ultimate, the uttermost extreme. The limit, beyond which none may ever travel.

Her nipples stiffened with breathless excitement. Nothing would ever be quite the same again.

Chapter Four

*T*he message had been perfectly clear.

OMEGA KNOWS THAT RICHARD CAN NEVER SATISFY YOU. TOMORROW, YOU WILL RECEIVE A BLUE ENVELOPE. OPEN IT, AND GO TO THE ADDRESS ON THE CARD INSIDE. IT IS TIME TO BEGIN YOUR EDUCATION.

Marcie jabbed angrily at the keyboard, determined that she was not going to go along with these infantile games. Work was not progressing as smoothly as she had hoped, and she wouldn't be able to get anything done this evening, even though Richard was away on business. Again. That was why he couldn't escort her to the dinner dance tonight.

At least, that was the excuse he gave. Marcie was pretty sure it was an excuse. Richard did not enjoy socialising, unless it was with a beautiful woman in a hotel bedroom, or at a stag night at his old school rugby club. That was why it was Alex, and not Richard, who would be escorting her to Grünwald & Baker's annual garden party that evening.

Richard might not be the most romantic of men, but then again, he was also one of the least jealous. Despite the attraction that held them together, he understood that in many ways he and Marcie were worlds apart. He didn't interfere in her life, and when he went out for the evening, Marcie never asked where he was going. She knew that if she asked him, he would tell her. But that would spoil the game, somehow. Maybe she just didn't want to know.

If Marcie wanted hearts, flowers and quick, hot sex on the back seat of a GTi, she had Alex. Slick, refined, ever-so-discreet Alex, with his Filofax and endless supply of fast cars. Alex, whose prick was always ready; Alex, who had for a time brought variety and excitement back into her life. Funny, that. Most of her friends thought of her life as incredibly glamorous, but it had become surprisingly humdrum in the last couple of years. Board meetings in which everyone was invariably out to get her; long days and nights spent alone, staring at an unforgiving computer screen; polite, civilised sex with Richard. All these things could pall. Even the money palled sometimes. Having everything you want doesn't always give you what you need. And she had needed Alex as much as she needed food or oxygen. The sex she enjoyed with him had become a drug.

In the beginning, it had been all sunshine and wonder, hot passion under the apple trees; lying naked in the yellowing corn, and thinking of nothing but the instinct for pure, sweet pleasure.

But was it enough any more? Pure pleasure,

like pure sugar, can cloy. The more refined the palate, the more piquant and subtle the dishes it demands. Richard was a dependable sex machine; Alex, a beautiful lover who anticipated her every need, her every whim. Both were more than happy to go along with whatever she wanted. Hadn't Alex even played the master-servant game for her benefit?

But these little games only served to intensify her hunger. Slowly but surely, dark desires and half-glimpsed cravings were taking over her life.

She saved copy onto the hard disk, printed out and switched off. Thank God, no more messages this time. She remembered the words blinking out at her from the screen that morning, *IT'S TIME TO BEGIN YOUR EDUCATION*, and her mouth went suddenly dry. Part of her was extremely irritated, part fascinated; and part afraid. The adventurous part of her wanted to know more. But there was no way she was going along with the charade. If the joker wanted to hang around waiting for her, he was going to have a long wait.

She closed the door and went upstairs to get changed. Alex would be here soon. Should she wear the red cocktail dress, or the silky blue top with the matching velour leggings? When she opened the wardrobe door, she was immediately drawn to the black stretch velvet mini-dress she'd bought a year ago, and never got round to wearing. It was a tart's dress, really; cut low in the neck and back, tight-fitting enough to leave nothing to the imagination; and cut high at the thigh. Maybe?

No, she couldn't possibly wear it. The chairman's wife would be there, a sour-faced woman of stern Baptist principles. Martha Stanhope-Miles detested her: she disapproved of absolutely every-thing about Marcie, especially her brains and the collection of degrees. Martha Stanhope-Miles believed that a woman's role was to support her husband through life like a dependable concrete bollard, and bask in the reflected glory of his success. At this thought, the unsuitable dress took on an enhanced allure. A wicked impulse made Marcie reach out and unhook it from the rail.

She slipped the dress off the hanger, and laid it out on the bed, ready to put on. As she was putting the hanger back into the wardrobe, she noticed a small velvet pouch hanging on a silk cord. She unhooked it, and pulled apart the neck of the bag, turning it upside down and emptying the contents into the palm of her hand.

The gleam of silver made her catch her breath.

A second silver clip, identical to the first, greeted her eyes. A tiny and exquisite instrument of pain and pleasure, engraved with a single Greek letter.

Omega.

Marcie shivered. Instinctively she tensed her fingers, and felt something crumple inside the bag. Trembling, she took the bag and a small piece of paper fell out. She smoothed it and read the message.

A WISE CHOICE, MARCIE. OMEGA IS PLEASED WITH YOU.

A mad, angry impulse made her pick up the dress and hurl it across the room. It hit the wall and slid down in a crumpled heap. Marcie sat down on the bed, her mind reeling.

Alex? No, don't be silly. Alex had been away in Edinburgh for the last week. She'd even called him there on the phone. He was driving straight here to pick her up. Richard, then. Surely Richard must be in on this. But no. She'd always been able to tell when he was lying. Besides which, he hated practical jokes and had absolutely no reason to indulge in this sort of torture. Richard was gentle, kind, undemanding, and inherently boring.

And it certainly hadn't been Richard that day on the train. Or in the darkened lift cage, suspended between floors.

The thought scared her. If it wasn't Richard – and she was sure it wasn't – someone had been inside her house, riffled through her clothes, violated her intimacy just as surely as the faceless man who had taken her in the lift.

This was getting beyond a joke.

A sudden thought hit her, and she pulled open the top drawer of the pine chest. The sweet fragrance of lavender floated out, but Marcie was not interested in sweetness. She rummaged through the underwear, looking for what she hoped would not be there.

Nothing. She breathed a sigh of relief. At least Omega had kept his hands out of here. And then she saw it, nestling at the bottom of the drawer, half-hidden by a pink lacy bra.

At first she couldn't work out what it was. A bewildering arrangement of black, shiny PVC straps, with a buckle. She picked it up, and saw the note underneath.

WEAR IT TONIGHT, MARCIE. YOUR OBEDIENCE IS PLEASING TO OMEGA.

She meant to take it downstairs, throw it away or burn it. But her anger turned to interest as she held this curious thing, realising with a gradual, fascinated repulsion what it was. She would throw it away in a little while. After she had tried it on.

Swiftly slipping off her panties. Marcie stepped into the harness, arranging the straps around her waist and buckling them tight. It was like a chic little chastity belt made of black PVC. One strap went round her waist, like a belt, and several more criss-crossed tightly over her hips. A final strap passed between her legs, and Marcie soon realised that this strap had a double purpose. It was not simply to cover the wearer's sexuality. It was designed to stimulate it. On the inside of the strap there were dozens of little spines made of flexible rubber. Spines that forced themselves between the wearer's sex-lips as she moved, causing the most exquisite sensations.

Omega must have known that she would try on the harness, known that once he had trapped her inside it, she would not have the will to take it off again. He had imprisoned her within her own sexuality.

Marcie turned to the mirror, and stood there for a moment, transfixed by the image of herself, naked save for the slender, shiny straps that encircled her waist and hips. She slipped a hand between her thighs, and pressed gently on the understrap. Immediately, a fire raged through her, inflaming her clitoris and filling her with wetness. She wanted so much to masturbate, to pleasure herself and ease the pain of her desire. And yet she suspected that no matter how often she climaxed, the desire for pleasure would never cease.

The chimes of the clock sounding the quarter hour brought Marcie back to reality. Alex would be here in less than half an hour. He mustn't find her like this. She took a last look at the harness. It would have to stay. She couldn't summon the willpower to remove it. It felt so wonderful, gently stimulating the sensitive flesh between her legs. To her surprise, she realised that her fears had turned to anticipation. There was a strange, wicked excitement in knowing that, beneath her velvet dress, she would be wearing the harness, and no-one would ever guess.

She got dressed quickly, piled her long red hair on top of her head and secured it with pins, leaving just a few wavy tendrils at the nape of her neck.

The doorbell rang. Alex was here already. Time to go. She glanced at the second silver clip, lying on the bedspread, and slipped it into her evening purse with the other. Better that Richard didn't find it if he happened to come home early.

Slipping her feet into a pair of high-heeled courts, she ran downstairs and into the welcoming arms of Alex Donaldson.

'Good evening, my dear. Not with your charming husband tonight?'

Martha Stanhope-Miles's smile was chilling, her eyes full of disdain. But her husband was eyeing Marcie's decolletage with obvious approval.

'It's good to meet you again,' Marcie lied, fingers crossed behind her back. 'Richard is away on business, I'm afraid. This is Alex Donaldson, a close family friend.' And then she added, 'Jeremy is always talking about you,' which was true. Jeremy Stanhope-Miles belonged to the 'my wife doesn't understand me' school of management, and was forever trying to bed any junior executives

– male or female – who would listen to his whining. The irony was that although he was definitely sweet on Marcie, she had always steadfastly repulsed his advances. She had no intention of sleeping her way to the top, even if that was what people bitched about her, behind her back.

She and Alex moved on across the extensive lawns towards the marquee, grateful to get away from Mrs Stanhope-Miles and her icy hospitality. She was only too aware that Martha was the source of the rumours about her, at least ninety per cent of which were untrue – though highly imaginative. Could Mrs Stanhope-Miles be the inspiration behind this hate campaign, too? No, no. Don't be bloody ridiculous, she told herself. There's a man behind all this, and you know it.

At that moment, Alex spotted someone he'd worked with on a reinsurance project, and made his excuses, leaving Marcie talking to a group of girls from the lower echelons of Purchasing. They were a giggly lot, mostly young and certainly very talkative. They only had one topic of conversation: sex.

'What do you reckon to that Gary Martin?' a blonde girl demanded, obviously viewing Marcie's opinion as an expert one.

'He's OK. Why?'

'He's been giving you the eye all evening, ever since you arrived!'

'You're joking.' Marcie glanced about surreptitiously, hoping to spot him without being spotted.

'No, it's true,' chipped in Sheila, a brunette with long red fingernails. 'He's over there, by the barbecue – talking to the tall bloke with the mousy hair. See him?'

Marcie looked towards the barbecue, and saw a dark-haired young man with olive skin and strong features. Gary Martin was universally admired at Grünwald and Baker, and legend had it that he was magnificently endowed, but Marcie had always made a point of avoiding him. There was something mildly threatening about him. Something that both attracted and repelled her. He'd tried to seduce her at the Christmas party. He'd been the worse for drink and she'd turned him down flat. He'd been quite unpleasant about it at the time, but since then they'd been on better terms. At least, she thought so.

She caught his eye, and turned away, heart thumping. What if Gary Martin was behind it all? The nasty little toerag! Should she march over there and confront him?

No, it was no good. The more she agonised about it, the less she knew and the less she understood. She was getting nowhere. Omega could be any one of a hundred blokes out there, and she wouldn't know any better. There was no sense in making a fool of herself. Better to keep her cool, pretend it didn't bother her. Besides, there was a certain excitement in the game. A big part of her didn't want the secret to end.

She left the group of office girls, and strolled past the barbecue, to take a closer look at Martin. He was looking at her intently, but as she walked past he averted his eyes.

'Hello, Gary. Enjoying yourself?'

He mumbled some sort of noncommittal answer, and turned away, clearly embarrassed. It was no wonder, really: his current girlfriend was hanging on to his arm, and was obviously wondering why her man was paying so much attention to Marcie.

Appreciative eyes followed her across the grass. The gazes felt like caresses on her flesh, flattering her just as the tight dress did, moulding and cupping every curve of her desirable body. It was good to feel desired, and Marcie felt very desirable indeed that evening. The harness chafed gently, seductively, between her thighs, and she knew that something must happen soon to relieve the terrible aching of her swollen clitoris.

She spotted Alex, and dragged him away from a group of admiring women. A band was playing in the marquee, so they drank more champagne and danced for a while. As they moved round the floor, Marcie felt Alex's desire for her, hot and strong, his body pressed up tight against hers. He was hard and more than ready for her. She looked up into his face, and the force of his desire seemed to burn into her through his clear blue eyes. He, of course, could have no idea of Marcie's torment. The spiked strap was grinding mercilessly into her most delicate flesh. No matter how she tried to avoid the delicious torment, there was no escape.

She had to fuck.

She slipped a hand between her body and Alex's, and began rubbing his burgoning hardness through the fabric of his trousers. There could be no doubt about what she wanted, what she was demanding; and he responded enthusiastically.

Alex bent forward and kissed the nape of her neck.

'Come with me.'

He took her by the hand and dragged her away,

out of the marquee and across the lawn towards the shrubbery.

'No, no, we can't!' Marcie giggled, wishing she hadn't had quite so much champagne. 'I only meant . . .'

But in her mind she was already astride her lover, straddling his nakedness, feeling him sliding up inside her. The shiny straps were biting into her, reminding her of her bondage to pleasure. But she couldn't let Alex see the harness! He'd demand to know the whole story.

She tried to drag him to a halt, digging her heels into the grass. It was dusk now. She hoped no-one could see them.

'I've changed my mind. Later, let's do it later. There'll be plenty of time after we get home.'

Alex turned and stared at her, obviously puzzled.

'What? Playing the little virgin? It's not like you, Marcie. I thought you were hot for me, darling.'

And, ignoring whatever interest the other guests might have in what they were doing, he picked her up in his arms and carried her off towards the bushes. Caught completely off balance, Marcie could only lie limply in his arms and let him do what he wanted to. Shouting would only draw attention, and there were enough rumours already, without giving Martha Stanhope-Miles more ammunition for her dirty tricks campaign.

The foliage was dense in this part of the walled garden. It was like being carried off into the jungle by King Kong. Marcie began to giggle and couldn't stop. She cursed the champagne, but already her sex was hot and wet. It couldn't be helped. It was too late to do anything about it now. Alex would just have to find out about the harness, and make of it what he would.

Panting with the exertion, Alex let go of her and she tumbled out of his arms onto the soft, powdery earth. High above, the first stars were just appearing in the navy-blue sky. The sounds of the party seemed as far away as the furthest star.

She reached up and pulled him down on top of her. His hot, heavy body almost crushed the breath out of her. Rolling sideways, she fumbled and found his flies. She tried without success to unzip him. Buttons! He was wearing button-fly trousers. Now, what serious Lothario wears button flies when he knows his lady's hot for his sex?

He was kissing her now, passionately and intensely; his tongue exploring the inside of her mouth with a gourmet's finesse. Spurning his attempts to help, Marcie worked on the buttons, returning his kisses as her fingers struggled to unfasten his flies.

At last she succeeded, and slid her hand inside. He was wearing silk boxer shorts, gaping open at the vent as his penis struggled to escape and reach its goal. She would help it to do just that. But first . . .

Marcie wriggled onto her knees and bent forward, pulling Alex's prick out of his trousers. She stroked it a little, admiring its smooth hardness, then pulled out his balls too, large and firm and full of spunk. He had obviously been saving himself for her. So she must reward him. Parting her lips, she engulfed his stiffness in her mouth, rejoicing in the salty taste of his clear love-juice, slippery and abundant on his swollen glans.

'Oh yes, yes!' Alex groaned beneath her, clutching her breasts and squeezing them in a frenzy of desire.

She sucked at him hungrily, letting her teeth graze gently over the flesh, turning her tongue over the glans and down the shaft, at first slowly and lasciviously, but with growing excitement. She cradled his balls, rejoicing in their heaviness: they would have plenty for her this evening, plenty of fountaining white joy.

Such power. Such delicious power to have a man in her mouth, completely at her mercy. At this precious, exultant moment, if she were to ask him for the world, he would grant her wish without a thought. For she was the guardian of his pleasure, its jailer and its saviour. She was his angel and his demon, free to choose his fate: salvation or damnation. Which would she choose?

She stopped toying with his shaft for a moment, and tightened her fingers on his balls, just hard enough to make him gasp with the discomfort. Marcie smiled to herself as she heard him groan, knowing only too well that his pleasure was heightened by the pain.

Alex was moaning now, softly and rhythmically; formless sounds whose only shape was their rhythm. Taking pity on him at last, Marcie began to fellate him again. They said that no woman could match a man's skills in fellation. Well, Marcie knew the head of this prick as well as if it had been her own. She knew exactly the tiny movements of lips and tongue and teeth which would provoke ecstasy or delay it indefinitely.

The game was an amusing one, but Marcie was hungry for her own pleasure. Her sex was pulsating gently with the need to be filled and caressed.

She sucked harder at Alex's swollen shaft. With a juddering sigh, he poured out his tribute into her triumphant mouth, then fell back, exhausted, onto the sun-warmed earth.

Marcie let him rest for a few moments, but not for long. One of Alex's major attractions was his quite remarkable virility. She had never known any man with the same capacity to regain an erection so soon after ejaculating. A few strokes of the hand, fingers tight around the base of his shaft, soon brought him back to rigidity. She wanted him so much, so much.

Alex's prick was well-formed and a little longer than the average; thick and with a bush of golden hair about its base. His balls were downy with golden curls; and the whole beautiful pleasure-ground had already been tanned a deep amber by the summer sun. In the bluish dusk, he looked like a beautiful statue, carved out of a pale sandstone, smooth and perfect. She stroked him gently, enjoying the feel of his strength, the curves of muscle on arms and thighs; the tautness of his belly, leading inexorably downwards.

With breathtaking suddenness, Alex stretched out his arms and grabbed her by the waist, catching her off balance and pulling her sideways. She tumbled willingly onto the soft earth, yielding with pleasure to his urgent desires. She had forgotten all about her guilty secret until his fingers began sliding up her dress, exposing her thighs and hips.

With an indrawn breath, Alex ran his fingers over the shiny black straps. He seemed captivated by her symbolic bondage, delighted by the tight straps that wove an intricate pattern across Marcie's firm flesh. A cage of shiny PVC enclosed all that he could ever desire.

He worked out quickly what the toy was for, slipping his fingers in between her thighs and working them upwards until they were sliding rhythmically backwards and forwards, pressing the rubber spines hard against her delicate womanhood.

Marcie longed to cry out loud, but her fear of discovery somehow prevented her, and she writhed soundlessly beneath her tormentor's skilful hands. She was in an agony of pleasure. Just when she thought she could take no more, Alex wrenched aside the strap between her legs, baring her martyred cunt.

He was inside her in an instant, thrusting past the tightness of the strap and into her throbbing wetness. She met his thrusts with eager upthrusts of her hips, taking him as far into her as he would go, feeling his bollocks slapping heavily against the entrance to her womanhood.

She came with gasps of pleasure, as he pinched and caressed her breasts. A flood of mingled sperm and cunt-juice inundated the harness, the hem of her dress, and the thirsty earth, which drank it down in eager silence.

She lay there for what seemed an eternity, scarcely aware that Alex had left her to fetch them some drinks. Her mind was still reeling from the excesses of her pleasure. Already the harness, now back in place between her thighs, was teasing her clitoris into urgent desire once again.

After a little while, she got to her feet and smoothed down her dress. No-one would ever guess what she had been up to. There was a wooden bench just in front of the bushes, and she decided to sit down on it and watch the fun whilst she waited for Alex to come back with the drinks.

Marcie was delighted to see that Mrs Martha Stanhope-Miles, town councillor, guardian of public morals and full-time busybody, was perilously close to being embarrassingly drunk. The fruit cup had obviously been her downfall: spiked with vodka and gin, every sip a mother's ruin. Martha was hanging on the arm of the delectable Gary Martin, who was not slow to take advantage of his position. If the Chairman's wife wanted to get friendly with him, he wasn't about to turn her away.

Her hand was sliding down his hip, edging its way, millimetre by millimetre, towards his swelling penis. If she hadn't been half-pissed, thought Marcie to herself, Martha would have been horrified to realise what her shameless hands were getting up to. The left one was on Gary Martin's pert backside now, pinching and squeezing the firm flesh under the tight fabric of his Chinos. Marcie giggled to herself, imagining how Martha would feel the next morning, when she realised what she had done.

Gary was well pleased. Martha wouldn't normally be his type, any more than he would be hers, but the word was that Jeremy Stanhope-Miles couldn't even raise a smile these days. Maybe that was why his wife always looked so sour-faced. Anyhow, if she wanted Gary Martin to ease her frustrations, that was just fine by him. He could be very discreet. What's more, he knew a thousand different ways to make her poor, unused body sing.

Still giggling, Martha allowed herself to be led away across the grass, towards the Hall. Lights blazed on the ground-floor of the house, but upstairs there were many darkened windows, many secluded corners where a man and a woman could get to know each other better.

Marcie wondered where Alex had got to with the champagne. Her eyes strayed to a little gaggle of typists, their tight mini-skirts no less tarty than her own, and their scarlet lipstick even more so. They were pretending not to notice the covetous gazes of the lads from the Overseas desk, and blushed and turned away as they drank in the lewd compliments. Marcie wondered what it would be like to be seventeen again – seventeen and pleasantly tipsy, on the verge of giving in to desire.

'All alone, Marcie?'

The whispered question came from behind her. Marcie swung round, but saw no-one. The dense foliage behind her seemed empty, unmoving.

'Has he left you all alone? I wouldn't leave a lady by herself, not if she had just given me such a beautiful fuck.'

Marcie wheeled round, but strong hands caught her by the shoulders, pressing her back down onto the bench.

'No, no. Don't turn round, Marcie. Keep looking ahead. I want to see your lovely, naked back. I want to caress your silken flesh.'

The voice was smooth and dark, like bitter chocolate. She realised with a shock that it wasn't the voice of the man in the lift, or the man on the train. It was strangely inhuman. Marcie longed to turn and look, but the hands held her in a grip of iron.

'What . . . What do you want from me?'

'To help you. To teach you. It is time to begin your education, you know that, Marcie. There is no time to lose.'

TIME TO BEGIN YOUR EDUCATION, MARCIE. TIME TO BEGIN.

Marcie's heart was thumping against her ribs, faster and faster. She no longer knew what she felt: fear or passion, excitement or terror. Perhaps a sprinkling of all these emotions.

The hands were caressing her now. She could have escaped, called out, tugged herself free of the insistent embraces. But to make a sound or a movement would draw attention to herself. Already she wondered what the other guests had noticed. They seemed to be showing no interest in her; they were a long way off; they were drunk; and yet . . .

She dared not move or make a sound, but she glanced down and saw the leather gloves, smoothing over the curves of her thighs, exploring the tops of her legs, as though instinctively drawn to the hot and fertile valley between them, still dripping with her own desire and Alex's. Still concealed and tormented by the spiked strap of the black PVC harness, her tormentor and her unseen lover. Could he know about it? Did he want to expose her shame to the whole world? He was easing up her skirt a little, the better to find his way underneath the tight, stretchy fabric.

Marcie stared at the gloves, in silent torment, half terrified, half elated. She had never seen them before, but knew what they signified; and they were exactly as she had imagined them: black, smooth, with a matt silken surface. And on the third finger of the left hand, a silver signet ring. A ring inscribed with a fimilar symbol.

Omega.

She shivered with anticipation as her thighs relaxed involuntarily, admitting the gloved hand to her innermost intimacy. An index finger pressed with cruel insistence along the line of the central strap, forcing the flexible rubber spikes against the tender flesh, awakening her once again to an agony of lust.

'You are an obedient pupil, Marcie. Omega will be pleased.'

She gasped as the pressure was released, and the finger slid out from between her thighs, and began to climb upwards, tracing the curves of thigh and hip, belly and bosom. The hand smoothed across her breasts, and she knew instantly what the touch signified. Fear and excitement clutched at her belly.

'Not entirely obedient, as I now see. You should not try Omega's patience, Marcie. You should not spurn Omega's gifts so callously.'

Marcie looked down to see the gloved hand pick up her velvet evening bag. Were none of her secrets safe any more?

'Let me help you with these, Marcie. Wear them with pride. They are the mark of Omega.'

She could not suppress a little cry as the hands roughly pulled down the fabric of her low-cut dress, exposing first one breast and then the other. The silver clips snapped shut on her nipples with rapacious eagerness, and she began to moan in soft, sweet distress.

'Remember, Marcie. You owe absolute obedience to the laws of Omega. We shall meet again, very soon.'

The whispered farewell lingered in Marcie's mind for many moments, as she mechanically cradled her breasts, their silver secrets concealed now beneath tight black velvet, only the faintest outlines remaining to betray the source of her inner turmoil. The pain and the pleasure were exquisite. She wanted to cry out and laugh, to tremble and to weep.

As Alex returned at last across the lawn, with a bottle of champagne and two glasses on a tray, she looked up at him with a face that was full of wonderment and desire; the face of one who has looked upon a new world.

'Take me home, Alex. Take me home and take me to bed.'

Chapter Five

The blue envelope arrived in the first post, just as the message had promised. She hesitated for a while, then threw it into the wastepaper basket with the rest of the junk mail. This so-called Omega wasn't going to get the better of her. If he thought he could make Marcie his plaything, he had another think coming. She went off and made herself and Richard a luxurious breakfast of croissants and honey, convinced that she had at last put the shadowy figure of Omega out of her mind once and for good.

Half an hour later, she retrieved the envelope and tore it open with trembling fingers.

It contained a black card, edged and inscribed with silver. Normally, Marcie would have thought it tacky; but recent events had taught her that the cliché of fear is no less terrifying than fear itself. The breath of Omega infused the very paper on which the silver characters shimmered, heavy with the scent of fear.

AT NOON TOMORROW, MARCIE.
THE HOUSE WITH THE RED DOOR AT THE
CORNER OF BACK CHURCH STREET AND
ABBOTS LANE.
OMEGA HAS SUMMONED YOU.

Marcie stared at the card in silence for a few moments, then slid open one of the kitchen drawers and dropped it inside. The drawer slid shut with a satisfying thud. Out of sight, out of mind. But as she walked away, the words resounded in her head.

OMEGA HAS SUMMONED YOU.

She spent the morning drowning her overactive brain in work. Things weren't going too well at Grünwald & Baker, all things considered. Of course, Jayne Robertson had succeeded in persuading the chairman that Marcie's cost-cutting measures were neither necessary nor likely to be effective. It wasn't difficult, seeing as Martha Stanhope-Miles had already had a good try at poisoning her husband's mind against Marcie. The managing director, Gavin, had been apologetic in the extreme; he knew only too well that the firm was facing rough times ahead. But it looked very much as if the young bucks on the Board were going to get their own way again.

Marcie felt doubly peeved. It wasn't the rejection: she could have coped with having her plans turned down, if they had been genuinely bad or unsuitable. What was really galling was knowing that the plans were exactly what Grünwald & Baker needed to pull it through the recession. Jayne Robertson was so bloody jealous that she couldn't see the wood for the trees: she was so

80

busy trying to prevent Marcie from taking her job, which ironically Marcie didn't give a stuff about anyway, that she couldn't see the truth. If Grünwald & Baker went down the tubes, Jayne bloody Robertson wouldn't *have* a job to be jealous about.

Neither will I, Marcie thought, prodding gloomily at the keyboard and calling up the graph of projected sales figures for the next six months. Grünwald & Baker were by far her most important clients. It didn't look good. And then, on top of it all, this bloody stupid Omega nonsense. She was convinced it was someone at the G & B office. But who? Who hated or desired her that much?

She had to find out who was behind it. And maybe the only way she was going to do that was to go along with the charade. Not for long: no way. She'd get out before things got beyond her control. She'd play along with it just long enough to find out the truth; and once she'd caught them out, she'd be able to lay the whole thing to rest.

She wasn't going to admit, even to herself, that the thought filled her not only with apprehensive dread, but also with excited anticipation.

'Marcie?'

Marcie rolled closer to Richard, and nuzzled into the crook of his arm.

'Hmm?'

He put his arm around her shoulders, drawing her into the warmth of his bronzed body, naked to the mellow summer sunshine. She could scent his sweat, tangy and exciting upon his golden skin, and a sudden desire overcame her. She wanted to lick this delicious, exhilarating cologne from his flesh, let the spicy flavours fill her mouth, rolling them around on her tongue.

'Marcie, I. . . How's Alex?'

It was an innocent enough question, but there was an unexpected hesitancy about it, as though it concealed another, unspoken question.

Marcie snuggled up closer. She didn't want to think about boring old Alex, not on a warm summer morning when there was no hurry to get out of bed.

'Oh, he's fine.'

There was an awkward silence for a few moments. Marcie knew what Richard was feeling and thinking. If he was at home a bit more often, had a bit more time for his wife, maybe she wouldn't need to fall back on this convenient little arrangement. It wasn't jealousy; no, not that. It was guilt. Here he was, married to the sexiest woman he'd ever met, the only woman who could turn him on no matter where, no matter when, and he was spending four nights out of five away on business.

She knew that this was what he was thinking, and sometimes she did feel pangs of resentment: she was no natural loner. She needed the company of men, and men evidently needed her: at any rate, she had no shortage of offers, welcome and not so welcome. She shivered slightly as the thought of Omega passed through her mind, a dark winged shadow flapping across a clear blue sky. She refused to think about such things on such a beautiful morning. There would be time enough to even the score with Omega.

Marcie was an infinitely practical woman. Richard loved his work, probably rather more than he loved her, and success for him meant being away from home more often than either of them would have liked. Well, she wasn't going to sit around brooding. If she couldn't have a full-time marriage, she would take her pleasures where she found them. That was where Alex came in. But she was tiring of Alex, despite his recent adventurousness. Alex would always be Alex: amiable and gentle and good-looking. No matter how hard he tried to play the cruel seducer, it would always be Marcie who called the shots.

'Marcie . . . have I been neglecting you?'

Before she had time to reply, Richard went on:

'Yes, of course I have. You're a sensual woman, Marcie. Beautiful and hot-blooded. And all I can do is leave you by yourself. If you get lonely, that's hardly a surprise.

'I want to treat you better, Marcie. Spend more time with you. Would you like to come away with me for a little while? I'm off on business up north today, and I've been asked to stay with Lord Thurlingham and his mother, the Dowager Duchess. I know they'd love to meet you. We could be back by Thursday. Grünwald & Baker won't miss you for a day or two.'

At the back of Marcie's mind, a voice hissed the previous day's warning.

AT NOON TOMORROW, MARCIE. AT NOON TOMORROW.

She rolled onto her belly, and propped herself up on her elbows, looking down into her husband's deep blue eyes. She planted a little kiss on the end of his nose.

'Sounds like fun. When do we start?'

Richard laughed delightedly, and grabbed her in

his strong arms, pulling her down so hard that she collapsed and fell on top of him. He kissed her passionately, his tongue probing between her willing lips and exploring the moist cavern of her mouth, still sweet and fragrant with fresh orange juice. Her whole body was as fresh and juicy as a ripe fruit, begging to be plucked.

He slid a knee between Marcie's leg, forcing her thighs apart. Her golden pubic curls were already dewy with moisture. She was hot for him, her desire overflowing the insufficient vessel of her womanhood.

Eagerly, Marcie pressed herself against Richard, delighting in the sensation of his hardness, swelling still against the base of her belly. She reached down, and managed to insinuate one hand between her belly and Richard's, burrowing downwards until she found what she was looking for.

Richard's balls were heavy with spunk, each one filling her palm. She caressed them knowingly, gently, with wicked skill; and was rewarded for her efforts by a tautening of the velvety purse. Then she slid her hand further between Richard's thighs, and began to toy with him, running the very tip of her fingernail in one lascivious sweep from his anus to the base of his balls. He groaned and submitted to her willingly, arching his back and spreading his thighs wide.

He reached up and began to play with Marcie's nipples, smiling with satisfaction as they grew ever-stiffer. He pinched them quite hard, and Marcie remembered with guilty pleasure the silver clips still lying at the bottom of her handbag, concealed but not forgotten. Even the memory of such piquant pleasure was enough to make her sex pulsate with frustrated desire.

Taking the initiative, Marcie spread her thighs and straddled Richard's hips. She took hold of his penis, and guided it towards the moist, hot cavern of her sex. He did not resist, longing only to feel himself slide into her as a dagger slides into its jewelled hilt.

Marcie tantalised him for a little while, revelling once more in the power of her own sexuality to enslave and enrapture. She placed the tip of Richard's swollen penis against the entrance to her secret cave, and ran it very slowly, very lightly, along the length of her crack. It was an exquisite sensation for them both. Marcie felt as though this smooth, eager penis was no more than a toy, an abject slave to her every desire. And if she chose to bring herself pleasure and yet deny it to her victim, well that was her prerogative as sex-queen and goddess.

Her resolve crumbled as Richard tweaked her nipples again, harder this time and with devastating skill. She engulfed him with one swift motion of her thighs, so hungry for him that she could no longer bear to tantalise herself with the silken touch of his glans brushing, light as a breath of wind, across her throbbing clitoris.

She rode him mercilessly, regulating the thrusts of his hips with her own weight and balance; refusing to allow him an orgasm until she chose to bestow pleasure upon him. But he had power, too: a subtle fingertip, inserted between cock and belly, was enough to bring Marcie to a sudden and very powerful climax. She fell forward onto Richard's belly, gasping with all the pleasure of submission to a greater skill. As she lay panting on his belly, Richard took the opportunity to awaken her desire once again, by gently biting at her nipples. She groaned with renewed lust.

But she soon got her revenge. For she began to ride him again, this time faster and faster, forcing him towards the heights of ecstasy, demanding his homage to her supreme artistry.

With a stifled sob, Richard let his pleasure fountain into her, unable to restrain his orgasm any longer. His spunk flooded her, and she sank, laughing with delight, onto his chest.

They lay together for some time, dozing in the morning sunshine, knowing that soon they would fuck again but not wanting to hurry the moment, not wanting to destroy the delicious intimacy.

Somewhere at the back of her mind, Marcie was trying to blot out the dark whisper, invading her thoughts with vicious insistence:

AT NOON TOMORROW, MARCIE. OMEGA HAS SUMMONED YOU.

She slid down the bed and fastened her lips on Richard's swelling penis. Nothing was going to spoil today. Nothing was going to get the better of Marcie MacLean.

They rode through the trees, sunshine dappling the horses' flanks with lime-green light. Marcie was glad she had agreed to come with Richard to Thurlingham Hall. It wasn't just that Lord Thurlingham and his mother had made them feel welcome; the Hall and its surrounding estate provided such a romantic setting. Rolling countryside surrounded the house, and crystal-clear trout streams trickled between the trees in shady forests.

She thought back to the previous evening, when she and Richard had sneaked off and made glorious love on the grouse moors, among the heather. It was such a pity Richard had to be so busy with business deals, Marcie mused, forgetting for a moment that this was supposed to be a working holiday. Heck, she'd even brought a briefcase full of reports to work on, if she got bored. Still, little chance of that.

Luckily, Lord and Lady Thurlingham had found plenty to amuse her during Richard's frequent absences. Catriona Thurlingham had taken her for long walks and shown her the historic sights in the nearby villages; and her son, Oliver, was an excellent horseman, as Marcie was discovering this afternoon.

'Tired out yet?' he called over his shoulder as they rode over the crest of a hill and back down into the woods.

'I'm fine,' Marcie panted, though truthfully she was exhausted. It had been years since she was on a horse, though she hadn't been a bad rider at school. But the years were taking their toll: she was using muscles she'd forgotten she had.

'Tell you what, let's stop for a breather over there, by the stream,' shouted Oliver Thurlingham, spurring his horse to a gallop. 'Race you there!'

He galloped off into the distance, and Marcie watched glumly as Tolly cleared the five-barred gate with ease. Should she try to follow, or should she take the sensible course of action, dismount and open the gate?

The sight of Oliver Thurlingham, grinning at her from the other side of the field, was sufficient to make her forget her years out of the saddle. The horse was strong and tall. It would get over the gate easily, especially if she took it at a slight angle.

The horse did clear the gate, with inches to spare. Marcie, however, did not. She hit the sun-baked ground with a dull thud, and lay there for what seemed an eternity, floating in and out of consciousness.

'Are you all right, Marcie? Oh God, Marcie. It's all my fault! I shouldn't have egged you on like that. Are you OK? Speak to me!'

Marcie opened her eyes and shook her head, to find herself looking up into Oliver Thurlingham's concerned brown eyes.

'It's OK. I'll live! But there'll be bruises tomorrow. My backside feels like it's been trodden on by an elephant.'

She tried to sit up, and found that she was dizzier than she had expected.

'Let me help you up,' Oliver said. 'We'll sit you down in the shade of the trees, over there by the stream.'

With no bones broken, but stiffer than she could remember ever having been in her entire life, Marcie accepted Oliver's proffered arm and allowed him to lead her across the parched grass into the shade of the trees, where he sat her down on a soft patch of grass beside the stream.

He moistened a handkerchief in cold water, and began undoing Marcie's blouse. Then he took a bottle of whisky out of his saddle-bag, and poured some of that onto the handkerchief as well.

'What are you doing?'

He laughed.

'You're scratched all over, Marcie. Just look at

yourself! We're going to need to bathe all those scratches, or they'll get infected.'

Marcie couldn't help thinking that Oliver Thurlingham was taking a more than solicitous interest in her scratches. Some of them were very minor indeed: even she could hardly make them out. But she submitted to his gentle touch, even allowing him to remove her bra and dab at the tiny lacerations on her breast. The whisky stung like hell, and she winced at the touch of the cold on her bruised and overheated flesh.

In spite of herself, she noticed with deep embarrassment that her nipples had stiffened appreciatively at Oliver's attentions. There was no doubt about it. He *was* a very good-looking man, no older than thirty-five at the outside, tall and slender with a touch of olive in his flawless skin. That would be from his Italian grandmother, mused Marcie. His features were aquiline and his eyes a very aristocratic grey. All in all, he was the very epitome of nobility. Hardly surprising, then, that Marcie was so attracted to him.

He was moving his attentions downwards now, tugging off her riding boots and then unfastening her breeches and easing them down over her hips. Usually quite brazen, Marcie actually blushed at the thought of revealing so much of herself to a virtual stranger, but made no move to draw away. She had not the will to deny him. He noted her reaction, and did not spare her modesty in any degree, pulling off her white cotton panties with expert ease.

Naked before Oliver Thurlingham, Marcie felt herself floating off into a near-dreamlike state. Perhaps the fall had stunned her more than she had thought? Perhaps the whisky that Oliver was forcing between her lips was going straight to her head? She felt lightheaded and frivolous, quite unable to resist whatever he might have in store for her.

Still gently but with great determination, Oliver pulled apart Marcie's thighs and began dabbing at the scratches between her legs, extracting the small thorns that had become embedded in her flesh.

'Poor Marcie,' he whispered. 'Such beauty. Such pain.'

The neat whisky burned like fire on her raw flesh, and for a moment when Marcie looked into Oliver's face she thought she saw a perverse pleasure there; a pleasure in pain.

His hand slid higher and higher up her thighs, and she simply lay there and let him do whatever he wanted. Her own desires were awakening now, and she could see the swelling outline of Oliver Thurlingham's penis, clearly delineated by his tight riding breeches. The thought that he wanted her filled her with excitement, and her sex began to pulsate to the secret rhythm of lust.

'Beautiful, suffering Marcie.'

His hand slid between the lips of her vulva, and she gasped as the whisky stung her most sensitive flesh.

In an instant, Oliver had taken the whip from his saddlebag, and was brandishing it in front of her. His face was a picture of crazed ecstasy, his prick now a threatening bulge in the front of his breeches. Marcie suddenly realised what he wanted, what would give him sexual pleasure, and, dazed though she was, she knew she would not submit to his perverse desire to hurt her.

90

Dragging herself to her feet, she pushed him away. To her surprise, he did not attempt to restrain her. As she thrust him away from her, she saw a genuine sadness in his eyes; the sadness of loss.

'Oh Marcie, sweet Marcie,' he breathed. 'If only you would let me show you the pathway to purest pleasure.'

For a moment, she looked into those eyes and was almost melted by their tenderness. Was this a crazed fool with a whipping fetish, or a misunderstood angel of desire, whose only mission was to bring her pleasure?

With a last effort of will, she gathered up her clothes and hurriedly dressed; then mounted her horse and galloped back over the moors towards Thurlingham Hall.

'It wasn't funny, Richard. It really wasn't!'

Marcie glared indignantly at Richard as he tried to suppress his laughter.

'Oh come on, Marcie, you've got to admit, it's a bit far-fetched. Wicked but handsome aristocrat undresses his victim and then pulls out a horsewhip!'

'Richard! You're making fun of me.'

'Sorry, sweetheart. Well, one thing's for sure: his sexual peccadilloes may be a little offbeat, but Oliver Thurlingham surely does have an excellent taste in women.'

Determined to be angry, Marcie threw a pillow at Richard's head. He ducked and made a grab for her, pulling her down onto the bed and pinning her there by her wrists.

'Want a ride, little filly?'

And he began to unfasten the buttons of her blouse.

It wasn't until the next morning, when she was getting dressed for a drive into the local town, that Marcie noticed the black card, edged in silver. It was underneath a plate on the breakfast tray that the maid had brought to her. Richard had left early for a business meeting.

She picked up the card with a trembling hand. The words glared out at her with apocalyptic rage.

YOU WERE NOT AT THE MEETING I HAD PREPARED FOR YOU, MARCIE. OMEGA IS DISPLEASED. OMEGA WILL TEACH YOU OBEDIENCE.

BE AT THE HOUSE WITH THE RED DOOR TOMORROW, AT NOON. TOMORROW AT NOON, MARCIE. DARE YOU BRAVE THE WRATH OF OMEGA A SECOND TIME?

Marcie lay in bed, wondering if she had been right to tear up the second card. If she had kept it, maybe it would have contained some clue to help her track down the mysterious Omega.

Richard was still snoring quietly by her side. She rolled over and looked at the clock. Three o'clock. In a couple of hours, it would get light. Even now, the sky was a fuzzy blue at the edges.

It was no good. She couldn't sleep. Sliding out of the bed as quietly as she could, she slipped her feet into her slippers and slung a light robe about her shoulders, then padded downstairs to the kitchen and clicked on the light.

She poured herself a glass of orange juice, and

went into her study. Maybe she could get a little work done.

The package lay on her desk, in front of the computer monitor. A gift-wrapped box, about six inches square, done up with metallic silver ribbon. Marcie stared at it blankly, its frivolous pink and silver wrappings strangely out of place amongst the debris of financial reports, statistical stables, computer diskettes.

She could ignore it. Turn back, go upstairs, go back to sleep. When she awoke, it would all be a dream, and she would no longer be afraid. The label teased her, just too far away for her to read the words. Perhaps she was just being silly. Perhaps Alex had left her a present before going off on his management course. Something silly and romantic; he liked to pamper her.

She peeled off the paper and opened the box. Inside, a layer of pink tissue paper obscured the contents. Underneath, something she didn't recognise: a small yellowish-white plug, smooth and innocent, like the stopper out of some primitive bottle. Carved ivory? It was certainly very old, for the silky surface was yellowed and criss-crossed with tiny veined cracks. She wondered what it could be for. Picking it up, she turned it over in her hand; a meaningless little trinket. Beneath it, half-hidden among the tissue paper, lay a small piece of paper.

THE PLAYTHING OF THE EMPRESS JOSEPHINE. FOR YOUR PLEASURE, MARCIE. FOR THE PLEASURE OF YOUR EXQUISITE ARSE. OMEGA WISHES IT.

For a moment, she did not quite realise what was being asked of her. No, not asked, demanded.

Then it hit her with a mixture of excitement and disgust. Omega, this infuriating charlatan who thought he could play games with her life, was asking her to masturbate with an ivory plug up her backside. And the Empress Josephine's arse-plug, at that!

The sheer preposterousness of the idea made her giggle, and she tossed the silly trinket into the air and caught it one-handed. But the idea made her shiver with excitement, too. She had never used such a strange prop before, and the notion held a certain perverse fascination. What would it feel like to be filled, stretched, violated in this most secret of places? She realised, to her immense surprise, that she was quite a prude at heart.

Well, why not? Why not sample the gift, since it had been given? No-one, not even Omega, would ever know whether or not she had submitted to temptation. It would be her secret, and hers alone. And perhaps the experience would not be entirely unpleasant.

There was a soft lambskin rug on the floor, near to the open window. A fragrant breeze was drifting in from the garden, carrying with it the scents of night-jasmine and damask roses, musky and sweet. A languid heaviness entered Marcie's soul, intoxicating and seducing with each perfumed breath. She took off her robe and let it fall to the ground in drifts of pale blue silk; then she stretched out on the lambskin, relishing the contact of the soft fleece against her tanned flesh.

The cool night-breeze wafted gently over her nakedness, teasing her nipples into firmness, awakening her senses to the imminence of pleasure. She drew up her knees, and her left hand slid surreptitiously beneath her buttocks, seeking the secret entrance to the last bastion of her womanhood.

The ivory felt cold and unyielding against her flesh, and she drew back, suddenly afraid to go on. But in spite of her fears her flesh was pulsating gently with the desire for release. She place the tip of her finger against her tiny, puckered hole and pressed gently. To her surprise, the flesh yielded instantly and her fingertip was swallowed up. A little harder, and her entire finger was inside the hot, moist tunnel. The sensation was not at all unpleasant; and yet, the plug was so much larger, so much thicker than a fingertip.

As though in a dream, Marcie tentatively pressed the tip of the ivory plug against the secret gateway. No, no; it was much too big! It would never go inside her without hurting her terribly. She would not do this thing.

The plug slid into her, her treacherous flesh yielding joyfully to the invader, swallowing it up and tightening around it with a new eagerness. Marcie gasped at the intensity of the sensation, quite unlike any she had ever known. And the fingers of her right hand slipped between her thighs, searching out the pulsating heart of her womanhood.

Her sex-lips parted to reveal the moist treasures of her desire, the perfect pink pearl within its fur-trimmed casket. Her middle finger slid into the slippery tunnel of her vagina, whilst her thumb began to stimulate her clitoris with delicate, rhythmic movements. It felt as though her body were independent of her will, her soul. Her hands seemed to be moving entirely of their own volition, her cunt and arse tensing in subtle harmony with each delicious stroke.

She was chasing pleasure now, glimpsing it far away in the perfumed darkness. Faster and faster she must race, or it would surely elude her. Her fingers toyed expertly with her flesh, stimulating it to new delights. She, not Omega, was mistress of her pleasure. And within seconds she welcomed her climax, falling back onto the lambskin rug with a great long sigh of ecstasy as the love-juices flowed more freely than ever before.

As she lay there on the rug, still dazed with the intensity of the sensations she had just experienced, a mechanical humming noise brought her back to her senses. A fax was spewing out of the machine, the sheets of paper curling down to the floor in a long scroll, huge letters ominous and black along its length.

YOU SEE, OMEGA KNOWS WHAT IS BEST FOR YOU, MARCIE. TOMORROW AT NOON. THIS TIME, DO NOT FAIL.

The house with the red door loomed above her, tall and imposing, its windows blank and enigmatic as they reflected the noonday sunshine. A smart Georgian house, three storeys high, in a quiet, residential part of town where there were few office workers or shoppers to see her as she stood there, desperate with uncertainty.

She glanced at her watch. Noon exactly. The sun was at its height, glaring down at this ludicrous escapade.

She put her hand into her pocket and touched the card, its two torn halves quietly malicious in the lining of her skirt pocket. How do you dress for a meeting with a man called Omega? The more Marcie thought about it, the more idiotic it all seemed. She had spent an hour just trying to decide what to wear: God knows, the guy could be any sort of weirdo, trying to lure her to her doom for all she knew. She was glad now that she'd left a note for Richard on the hall table, giving him the address of where she'd gone. If all went well, she'd be back home before he found it.

Marcie raised her hand and, obeying a sudden impulse, pressed the brass doorbell. A distant ringing told her that it was working. But no-one came. She tried again, pressing her ear up against the door; but not a sound came from within.

No-one at home? So she'd come here on a wild goose-chase. So much the better, in retrospect. There was no harm done. She could turn round and go back home: bake a cake, weed the garden, have a shower, feed the cat: in short, get back to normality. She'd exorcised the demon, and found it was nothing more than an elaborate hoax. She could have laughed out loud with relief.

But something made her lift her hand to the door-knocker. She ought to try just one more time. As her fingers touched the brass lion's head, the heavy door creaked and suddenly swung inward on slightly-rusted hinges.

She blinked for a few moments, unaccustomed to the sudden twilight which reigned within the house. Heavy brocade drapes lined the hallway, cutting out much of the sunlight from the small windows. Half terrified and half intrigued, Marcie stepped inside.

It was an ordinary house, though rather old-fashioned. She felt quite disappointed really – it wasn't the Addams family residence, by any means. She scanned the hallway quickly. No dust anywhere – so the place was inhabited, despite the time-warp look.

'Anybody at home?'

Her voice echoed up the stairwell, but no-one answered.

'Hello?'

Nothing. Either she was alone, or this was a still more elaborate charade than she had thought. The door had been left open on purpose, that was for sure: it was on the latch. So she was evidently expected. She wondered what to do: go home, or go inside. Cautiously, she pushed the door to, making sure to leave it on the latch just in case. . .

The tiled hall echoed to the click-clack of her court shoes. She wondered why she hadn't worn something a little more sensible – something she could run in. At the end of the hall were three doors – one on either side and one directly in front of her. Two were closed, but the door on her right was slightly ajar. Was it a sign, perhaps? Or a trap?

She decided to ignore the half-open door and went straight ahead, pushing the door open quickly and hanging back, in case someone or something was behind it, waiting to pounce on her.

The room she walked into was in darkness, save for a single oil lamp with a red chenille shade, standing on a table in the middle of the room. Heavy drapes were pulled across the windows, and the only light was the red glow from the lamp. Marcie knew it was madness to enter, and yet she stepped forward slowly, tremulously, darting glances to right and left. Every shadow seemed to contain a sinister shape, a glittering pair of eyes or sharpened teeth.

There was an envelope on the table in front of the lamp. A black and silver envelope. Hands trembling, she opened it and held the card up to the feeble light.

A GIFT FOR YOU, MARCIE. TAKE IT WITH YOU ON YOUR JOURNEY.

Marcie looked down, and saw a black and silver label hanging from the handle of a tiny drawer in the table. She pulled on the handle and the drawer opened.

The curls of black leather gleamed in the rose-red lamplight, unreal and strangely friendly in the rosy glow. Marcie reached in and picked up the object by its handle. Immediately it took on a new and far more daunting aspect. A cat-o'-nine-tails, each leather lash tipped with a small knot. An instrument of pain.

And pleasure.

What did Omega intend by this? Did he intend her to harm herself? She was revolted by the idea. The silver clips had been one thing, but this was quite another. The small and rather insignificant pain which the clips had inflicted had been easily transformed into the glow of pleasure. But the thought of the lash, biting into her delicate flesh, made her tremble with a terrible, fascinated revulsion.

Journey? What journey did Omega intend her to make? Absently, she clutched at the whip-handle and took a few steps towards the door to the next room. At least the whip would serve as a weapon, should she be attacked. Its shaft felt warm and alive in her hand, an outgrowth of her own anger, her desire for justice and revenge.

She passed through the door, hardly afraid now, paying little heed to the dangers that might lurk within the next room.

It was empty, and very dark. Once again, a single lamp burned on a small table, above a black card with silver writing.

THE NEXT ROOM, MARCIE. YOUR DESIRES SHALL BE SATISFIED.

It was a trap. It must be. Someone was waiting in the next room, waiting to do her unspeakable harm. She must turn back, now, before it was too late. Got to get out of this nightmare, back to the sunlit world of ordinariness and cosy reality.

Still clutching the whip-handle, Marcie walked on across the room, and pushed open the door.

She blinked in the suddenness of the light, her eyes unaccustomed to the ferocious brightness; and she almost fell down the half-dozen stone steps which led down into a sort of basement room. The room was inhospitable and window-less, a bare stone floor and peeling walls that might once have been painted a chill pale green.

The light was coming from perhaps two hundred candles, arranged in wrought-iron candelabra all over the room: hideous, blackened candelabra fashioned into bizarre, twisted shapes, some grotesque in their suggestiveness, others simply stark and forbidding.

And in the centre of the room hung a man: naked and gagged, suspended by his chained wrists from an iron hook in the ceiling. His feet barely touched the floor, and he struggled to keep his balance. As he saw Marcie enter the room, his eyes widened in terror. She realised that she was still holding the whip.

Her first impulse was to find a way of rescuing the man, but how? His wrists were in manacles, no doubt locked and certainly securely chained to the ceiling. She could have removed the gag from his mouth, but what good would that have done? He would only cry out in his pain and fear, and she would be powerless to help him. And there was something so very appealing about his helpless nakedness, strung up and entirely at her mercy.

She walked down the steps into the room. The heat from the candles was overpowering, like a slap on the face. She was too hot, much too hot. As she got closer to the man, she saw that his bronzed, muscular body was covered in little beads and trickles of sweat. How good it would taste to lick off that sweat, as she had licked off Alex's.

She stood before the man and reached out her hand, wonderingly, to touch the glistening flesh. A strange satisfaction rippled through her as she saw him flinch, trying to edge away from her yet completely unable to do so. His weakness excited her, inflamed her lust. She wanted to feel her power over him.

His prick was substantial, even in repose. For the first time in her life, Marcie had a man truly at her mercy, his body open and exposed for her to do exactly what she wanted to it. Would she bring him the gift of pleasure, or the gift of tears?

A half-smile playing about her lips, Marcie unfastened the button on her skirt and tugged down the zip. The leather skirt fell to the floor with a gentle swish. Underneath she was bare-

101

limbed, wearing only a small pair of lacy panties. Would her victim like her to take off those panties, show him what was inside? He was watching her intently now.

She tormented him for a while, sliding her hand down inside her panties and stroking her pubis provocatively. To her surprise, her victim's cock did not respond. Perhaps he needed stronger persuasion.

Marcie pulled down her panties and stepped out of them. She pressed the fragrant gusset up against her victim's face, making him breathe in the sweet odours of talc and sex. He groaned faintly, but did not respond as Marcie had hoped he would.

She sat down with her back to the wall, in full view of her victim, and spread her legs wide. The blaze of candles left nothing to the imagination, and she was well aware of the effect she must surely produce: naked from the waist down, with her long legs spread wide to reveal the treasures of her womanhood.

Picking up the whip, she ran its many leather thongs lightly over her flesh, teasing nipples and belly and thighs. Then, on a sudden whim, she reversed the whip so that its handle was pointing towards her, and pressed the tip of the handle against her tight, wet sex.

'You see?' she taunted him. 'I don't need you. I don't need any man.'

The whip-handle disappeared inside her cunt in a single, smooth thrust. The intensity of the pleasure it produced surprised even Marcie, and she stayed still for a moment, just enjoying the sensation of delicious fullness.

But she could not resist the temptation for long.

Soon, she began to ram the whip-handle into her soft, wet sex, again and again; faster and faster, and all the time staring into that wide-eyed, frightened face.

Her pleasure came quickly, and she fell back panting against the wall. To her annoyance, her victim's prick was still disappointingly flaccid. And yet, as she rose to her feet, she was sure that he wanted her.

The whip twitched in her hand. It was an instinctive gesture, as natural as breathing. Without thinking, Marcie raised her arm and brought down the lash, rather tentatively, upon her naked victim's flank. The many shiny thongs uncurled like greedy tongues upon the glistening flesh, and Marcie looked on in a terrible fascination.

The blow was a light one, but the man writhed beneath the lash. He could not cry out for the gag filled his mouth, but he began a low moaning, and his eyes widened with fear.

A wild lust took hold of Marcie, warming her belly, putting a ferocious strength into her arms. A distant voice – was it a real voice, or was it inside her head? – was calling to her, urging her on. The lash fell again and again on the glistening flesh, raising dark red welts on the firmness of back and buttocks. And Marcie's victim writhed and moaned in his torment.

At the very first stroke of the lash, his prick began to twitch into life, uncoiling like a sleepy serpent, suddenly awake and ready for the kill. Each successive blow seemed to endow it with greater life, and Marcie's own excitement grew as she realised her power over this unknown sacrifice. His balls were taut and heavy, his shaft straining for the release that only torment could bring.

As his spunk fountained from his cock in thick white jets, Marcie tore open her blouse, and felt the hot fluid spurt over her breast. The tribute had been paid, and the sacrifice was complete at last.

As she walked back up the steps, into the darkened house, she did not even bother to glance behind her.

Chapter Six

Marcie sank onto the taxi seat with a sigh of relief, and threw her briefcase onto the floor.

'Waterloo Station, please.'

They drove off into the afternoon traffic, dodging the pushbike couriers and dozy pedestrians whose brains had been fried by the relentless sunshine.

'Drop me off at the Elephant, would you?' Greg Baxter leaned forward and instructed the driver. He turned to Marcie and smiled, that same dazzlingly heroic smile he'd inflicted on everyone at the meeting. 'Friends again?'

'Honestly Greg, I don't know why I agreed to share this cab with you. Would have served you bloody well right if I'd slammed the door and left you standing there.'

'All's fair in love and corporate finance, Marcie. I thought you were supposed to be a professional.'

'Pity you're not, then,' Marcie observed. 'A logical argument is one thing, bloody-mindedness is another. Did you have to oppose everything I said, just for the sake of it?'

'I just didn't think you'd got the figures right, that's all. But you've got one figure that's absolutely spot on.'

'Sleazebag.' She wriggled out of his reach, shifting her leg so that his hand slid off her black-stockinged thigh. Alarm bells were ringing at the back of her mind. Could Greg Baxter be the man behind the Omega scam? He had the right sort of adolescent mentality, that was for sure. And rumour had it that he had some pretty specialised sexual tastes, too. But if he really was Omega, why would his behaviour be so gross, so obvious? The man behind Omega had style and intelligence – enough intelligence to have worked out how to hack into her 'secure' computer terminal. No, it couldn't be Greg Baxter, surely. On the other hand, he had been half-heartedly trying to seduce her for months, with such automatic regularity that the whole thing had lost all its threat and degenerated into a game.

Only now she wasn't so sure it was a game any more.

She dropped Greg in the concrete wasteland outside Elephant tube station, and glared at his back as he disappeared into the ticket hall. Omega or not, he was a bloody nuisance, and she could have done without his opposition at the meeting. Why had he been so bloody-minded, so gratuitously awkward? He could see that she had got her facts straight. If he hadn't mobilised the rest of the board against her, she could have got the plans through to trial stage that morning, and then *everyone* would have seen that she knew what she

106

was talking about. Good God! She'd won them the Bermuda deal last year, what more proof did they want?

Jayne Robertson had been particularly malicious, even worse than usual. It was perfectly clear that Jayne loathed Marcie, and the reasons weren't hard to identify. Ten years older than Marcie, she was hanging onto her seniority by a thread. She was less able, less authoritative, less knowledgeable, and she knew it. She felt threatened, and nothing Marcie tried to do made any difference. Ever since the day when Marcie had first set foot in the head offices of Grünwald & Baker, Jayne Robertson had done everything in her not-inconsiderable power to make her life a misery.

Ironically, it had been Jayne who arranged for Marcie to work from a home base, arguing that telecommuting was the future of the industry, and would give Marcie greater freedom. It was a load of balls, of course: a shit-hot management consultant was the last person Jayne wanted around, poking a nose into all her little 'systems'. No, she'd just wanted Marcie out of the way: off-site, and well out of the formal career structure. Ironic, then, that the arrangement suited Marcie down to the ground.

Of course, most of all, she'd wanted Marcie away from Stanhope-Miles. For some reason best known to herself, Jayne Robertson was obsessed with the company chairman. It wasn't just the obvious reason; it didn't seem to be his power that turned her on.

But turned on she was. Marcie recalled that afternoon, six months ago, when she had been working late in the computer room at Grünwald &

Baker. She'd been using only a small desk lamp, so she supposed no-one had realised she was in there. When she got up to leave, at around quarter to eight, all the offices were in darkness and the night-lights were on in the corridors, making the place seem like a macabre underground bunker. She'd hurried down the corridor towards the lift, anxious not to get locked in when the security guards did their eight o'clock rounds.

Just as she was approaching the lift doors, she heard noises coming from the direction of the Sales Director's office. She knew Simon was away on business in Scotland, and she'd noticed his personal secretary leaving for home at five-thirty, with everyone else. There really ought not to have been anyone in that office.

She knew she ought to call Security, get someone up here who knew what he was doing. It might be industrial espionage, or simple burglary. Either way, it would be foolish to get involved in something she might not be able to get out of. But maybe she'd just take a quick look first, to make sure she'd got her facts right: she'd look pretty silly if it turned out to be a couple of cleaners, working late.

On tiptoe, she approached the door of the Sales Director's office. It was very slightly ajar, and through the inch-wide gap Marcie could see a glow of light coming from the inner office. The outer office, where the secretary worked, was empty.

Cautiously, she pushed open the outer door, just enough to slip inside. To the right of her, the door to Simon's private office stood half-open, and she held her breath, terrified that she would be caught. Voices were drifting out of the inner office, whispers and hysterical giggles, mingled in an intoxicating cocktail. She thought she recognised the voices, but how could she be sure?

Very, very slowly, she edged nearer to the door and flattened herself against the wall, then glanced into the inner office. She need not have worried about being noticed: the couple inside were far too interested in each other to take any notice of anyone else.

Jayne Robertson was lying across Simon's desk, her skirt up around her waist; her slender naked thighs eerily pale in the fluorescent light. Her head was hanging down, her long brown hair untied and falling in a glossy curtain, almost to the carpet. Her eyes were closed but her mouth was open, and she was giggling and sighing. Stanhope-Miles was pumping into her, still fully dressed save for his naked cock and balls, which he had pulled out of his designer pants to service his mistress of the moment. He was groaning quietly to himself as he thrust into her, and was quite oblivious of everything around him.

Marcie watched in silence, mesmerised. She had always thought Jayne Robertson's interest in her boss had been one of deep respect, reverence even. But now she knew the true depth of Jayne's feelings, and it was a real revelation. And what of all those rumours about the Chairman's virility, or lack of it? She thought of poor stone-faced Martha Stanhope-Miles, and mused with grim humour that Martha had probably arranged the whole liaison for her own convenience. Twenty years of Stanhope-Miles's dead weight on top of her entitled her to a reprieve.

Another sight disturbed Marcie. The filing cabinet was open, and the desk on which Jayne was writhing was strewn with confidential files. Stanhope-Miles might be entitled to have access to the files, but certainly not Jayne Robertson. It was inconceivable that Simon would have gone away and left those files in his office for anyone to see. What's more, his super-efficient secretary was obsessive about security matters. Marcie looked on and could not, or refused to, understand.

It wasn't until a few weeks later, when Simon was eased out of the company in a skilful bit of boardroom manoeuvring, that Marcie realised what had been going on. That night in the office, Simon had been officially killed. And Jayne and Stanhope-Miles had been fucking on his grave.

That had been just the beginning of the unpleasantness, mused Marcie. And it wasn't just Jayne and Stanhope-Miles who were involved in it. Graham Elderton, Jon DaSilva, Sadie Price, Ian Hamilton: they had all quite clearly been involved in getting rid of people who, for some reason or another, didn't quite fit in at Grünwald & Baker. Marcie was beginning to wonder if she was next.

The cab swung into the forecourt of Waterloo station, and she got out, paid and stalked off up the steps.

'Ere, darlin'. What's a sexy little lady like you doin', lookin' so dahn?'

She turned round to see the cab driver smiling at her. He wasn't bad-looking: quite young, and nicely bronzed in his sleeveless T-shirt.

'Bet you could fancy a bit of rough, eh? Why not jump back in? I could show you a good time.'

More tempted than she would dare admit, Marcie closed her ears to his words and quickened her pace, half-running up the steps past the down-and-outs with their predatory smiles and grasping hands. It was like going back out of the honesty and clarity of the sunshine, into the cold darkness of a world in which she could no longer recognise herself.

What was she doing? What was she becoming? She looked over the past couple of weeks, and seemed to be recalling a bizarre dream-sequence from a *film noir*. She had walked through the gate into a dark underworld, where inexplicable acts were the only exorcism of unacceptable desires.

As she closed the train door and sat down, she remembered the young man, faceless and helpless, hanging limply from his chained wrists, his flesh seared and reddened from her assaults upon him. Why had she struck him with the whip? What violent impulse had driven her? As the scene filled her mind, the emotions came flooding back, the overwhelming lust for the sweetness of pain and domination. Feelings which Omega had released. Knowledge which she had not known she had.

What was happening to her? What was Omega doing to her mind, to her body? The simplicity of sex was becoming transformed into a dark, seductive world of subtle torment. A delicious addiction, quickly acquired but not so easily broken.

'Good afternoon, Mrs MacLean.'

The Colonel doffed his hat, respectful to a fault as he always was. Was that a knowing gleam in his watery blue eyes? Marcie dismissed the thought as paranoia. Ever since she and Alex had made love, with such naked abandon, in the orchard, she had worried about just who had seen what they had done. Rumours spread like wildfire in a village. There had been one or two comments, one or two obscure, veiled remarks which might or might not mean anything.

'Good morning, Colonel. How are you?'

'Much better for seeing you, Marcie. We haven't been seeing so much of you lately.'

'Oh, I've been away on business,' Marcie replied hastily. 'And Richard is often away. I'll be seeing you later.'

The key turned in the lock, and she stepped into the coolness of the hallway. The only sound was the reassuring tick-tock of the grandfather clock, marking off the seconds until the evening, when Alex would come and ease the tedium of her solitude.

She kicked off her shoes, peeled off her dress and stepped into the shower. The needles of icy water awoke every nerve-ending in her body, driving her into a hyper-consciousness she sought only to shun; and she began to moan, very quietly, very gently, for a comfort she dared not seek.

Marcie enjoyed living in Littleholme, but sometimes it felt as if a thousand eyes were on her. Everyone wanted to know your business, not like in a city where you were just a number, just a cipher. Here, you mattered to a sometimes alarming extent. Marcie thought back to the anonymity of that day in the darkened lift cage, where she had become the ultimate slave to passion. Not just other people's, but most of all her own. No will, no responsibility, no thought.

The ultimate nothing.

And at that moment, nothingness seemed almost welcoming. Even the fear did not seem to matter. To surrender herself, like a helpless child, into the arms of a greater will, a greater passion, seemed the only worthy ambition. Sometimes, thought was nothing more than pain; and pain could be the most exquisite of pleasures.

After dressing, she picked up the post, poured herself a drink and went out into the garden. The heat hit her chilled flesh like a solid wall, and for a moment her head reeled. In the distance, the little brook at the bottom of the orchard was trickling noisily over smooth stones. Beyond the trees, she could just make out the angular figure of Deanna Miles, parish councillor, local author and general busybody, ostensibly watering her hanging baskets, but clearly on the look-out for any scandal or gossip. Well, she would have a long wait today.

Marcie sat down on a sunbed and opened the first of the envelopes. Nothing more exotic or terrifying than a gas bill. Her subscription copies of *Forum* and *Pleasure Principles*; she put them to one side, for bedtime reading. Maybe she and Richard could pick up a few tips.

The last envelope was A4 size, plain and brown. It had no postmark, just a Mailsort code. Junk mail, evidently. She was going to throw it away unopened, but on an impulse she tore it open and pulled out the contents.

It was a fetishwear catalogue, glossy and garish. The cover depicted a vampish woman in a black leather basque, pierced to allow the breasts to poke through, stiff-tipped and threatening. Marcie noted with a shudder that the woman's red-painted nipples had been pierced with little silver rings, linked by a heavy silver chain which distended them.

She turned the page, and entered a whole new underworld she had scarcely imagined existed. A world of master and servant, mistress and slave. On the facing page, a woman in a tight rubber dress and spike-heeled platform boots was dragging along a hapless young man, dressed in nothing but a tiny leather posing pouch, utterly helpless to resist, since she had him fast by the thick brass chain about his slender neck. His mistress's expression was one that Marcie had never seen before: a grotesque mixture of hatred and devotion.

Turning the page, she found pictures of naked men and women, bound with leather thongs; masters and mistresses in leather, rubber and PVC, masked and threatening; boots and masks and harnesses just like the one she had worn on that fateful night at the garden party. As she looked at the pictures, she felt a wave of longing wash over her. A great longing to be part of this world where servitude was safety. To be mistress or servant? Somehow, it did not matter any more. Simply to be redefined and set free.

The sound of the doorbell called her back to reality. She glanced at her watch: three-thirty. She wasn't expecting anyone. After working into the early hours the previous night, and the meeting this morning, she had promised herself a quiet afternoon and then a night of fun with Alex. With a groan, she swung her legs off the sunbed and went to answer the door.

Outside the back door stood the slender, black-leather-clad figure of a despatch rider, his face completely obscured by a black helmet and tinted visor. He was carrying a box and a clipboard. As she signed for the parcel Marcie glanced towards his bike, noticing with surprise that it did not carry the name of any courier service. And he had parked it down the side of the cottage, in the secluded yard, as though he wanted no-one to notice it there.

She handed the clipboard back to the silent courier, accepted the parcel and stepped back to close the door. But the biker stepped forward, taking her by surprise, pushing her further back into the hall.

He clicked the door shut behind him. They were alone in the silent house.

'What do you want?' Marcie wanted to run away, but his leather-gloved hand was on her arm; not holding her fast or restraining her, simply touching her bare flesh. That touch electrified her; and the scent of leather and sweat and two-stroke intoxicated her with sudden desire.

There was a face behind that perspex mask; a face and eyes. Were the eyes cruel, gentle, knowing, stupid? Marcie no longer sought to know. She was speechless with fear, desire, excitement.

When his hands began undressing her, she wanted to cry out with elation, yet she was afraid, too; afraid that this silent man meant her real harm. So she submitted to his urgent desires obediently, almost impassively, as though she felt nothing, when all along her body was a seething mass of unsatisfied desires, bubbling to the surface like marsh gas in some dark, mysterious fen.

Her nakedness evidently did not displease him, for he ran his hands all over her body. The contact of the leather, supple yet harsh, made her moan with pleasure, and her nipples rose up in homage

115

to this strange lovemaking; hard, rose-pink crests of treacherous pleasure.

Naked, she felt doubly vulnerable beside this strange, robotic figure in its prison of leather and perspex. Was there really a man inside the sinister black suit? Did the faceless visor conceal emptiness? Was she being seduced, perhaps, by some beautiful, lascivious android?

The very thought of it dampened her crotch, made her breathing harsher and more shallow. Were there metal claws, instead of fingers, inside those shiny black gauntlets? She shivered as she imagined the metal skeleton beneath the leather skin, like a strange insect or deep sea creature within its carapace. Metal claws, crawling over her naked flesh, exciting her, possessing her.

She reached out and drew down the zipper on the biker's leather trousers. He made no attempt to prevent her; and she slipped her hand inside his flies. Inside, he was naked: nothing between hot flesh and warm leather. Her hand met the upward curving shaft of his penis, and grasped it firmly. It was pulsating with vibrant life. She pulled it out, and saw that it was as beautiful as it felt: smooth and thick and long, with a glistening, rounded head. She wanted so much to lick it, suck it, taste the milk of life as it flooded her greedy tongue.

But as she bent down to suck him, he pushed her away. He had other plans for her.

The biker opened the back door, flooding the cottage kitchen with sunshine. He seemed even more unreal than ever, his leathers gleaming in the sudden light, his cock a sculptured ivory against the black leather. Then he gripped Marcie's wrist and led her outside, into the unforgiving daylight.

'No! I can't! Someone will see.'

She tried to wriggle free, but it was useless. He was inexorable, unstoppable.

Trees and bushes shielded the little yard from the road, and screened it from the rest of the garden. Normally, this was where Richard tinkered with the kit-car he was building, but at the moment it was over at the garage, having some professional work done on the braking system. Marcie darted anxious glances around her. Was she safe from discovery? Could those few trees and shrubs really conceal the indecency of what she was doing from prying village eyes? Strange that at a time like this she was thinking of her reputation, rather than her safety. She thought of Mrs Miles, vigilantly watering her hanging baskets, and groaned inwardly. If there was anything to be seen, she would be sure to see it and report on it to the rest of the village.

But her thoughts did not dwell on privacy for very long. The biker had plans for her. His Harley-Davidson gleamed in the afternoon sunlight, superb shiny chrome and well-polished leather, resting on its stand. The scent of engine oil thrilled Marcie as she ran her fingers over the sun-warmed seat.

The biker pushed her gently towards the bike, until her back was up against the back wheel. At first she did not understand what he wanted her to do; then realisation struck. Silently, he lifted her up by the waist and pulled her legs apart, sitting her astride the seat, back to the handlebars. Then he laid her down gently, until her head was on the tank; and with little lengths of cord tied her wrists loosely to the handlebars.

The biker's cock was inside her swiftly and efficiently, and he began to thrust in and out of her like a piston moving up and down inside a well-greased cylinder. His cock was silky-smooth in the soft wetness of her womanhood; and she responded to each thrust with a movement of her hips. They fucked together with rhythmic, well-oiled precision.

Now she was a part of the machine, too. A machine for riding, just like the Harley-Davidson. She gazed up into the sky, and the sunshine blinded her like the reflections from well-burnished chrome.

She came with a cry she could not suppress: a cry of ecstasy unbound, arching her back the better to accept the tribute of his foaming seed.

He came silently, only the faintest shudder betraying his pleasure. Beneath him, Marcie lay moaning, writhing in her ecstasy, the willing victim of her own dark desires.

Later he untied her and rode away, melting like a phantom into the lengthening shadows of evening.

Alex drove her to the airport the next morning. Richard, of course, was far too busy with an 'important client' to see his wife off on her business trip.

'I'll pick you up on Saturday. Have a good trip, sweetheart.'

Marcie returned his chaste kiss and opened the car door. She thought about telling him everything, but something stopped her. She smiled, got out of the car and walked towards the check-in desk.

The trip to Berlin was an unexpected treat, or a damn nuisance, depending on how you looked at it. Marcie could have done without it. She needed to get to the bottom of this Omega thing. She needed to do something about the hostility at Grünwald & Baker. What she didn't need was two days abroad, trying to clinch a deal that wouldn't even have been necessary if Greg Baxter hadn't been so bloody difficult.

When the plane landed at Templehof Airport, Marcie got into a taxi and drove straight to the hotel, a four-star glass and chrome monstrosity off the Kurfürstendamm. She had the rest of the day to kill: the interview with Herr Niedermayer wasn't until the following morning.

She began to wish she had tried harder to persuade Alex to come along. At least she wouldn't have been so lonely. Berlin was supposed to be the fun-palace of Europe, now the wall had come down; but she didn't expect to see much night-life. Maybe she'd go and see a movie, go to the theatre? Whoopee! Welcome to the pleasure-dome.

She ate a solitary dinner, read a magazine, got bored. Maybe it wouldn't be safe for a lone woman to go drinking in a bar? She was just about to give up and have an early night when the phone in her room rang.

'Frau MacLean?'

'Yes.'

'There is a visitor for you. Shall I send him up to your room?'

'I. . . Yes, all right.'

119

It'll be the Berlin representative, she thought to herself. Stanhope-Miles mentioned he might be making contact.

She got her papers out, tidied herself up, and a few minutes later there was a knock on the door.

'Komm.'

The door opened, and Marcie drew back in sudden alarm. As she stepped back towards the window she glanced down at the street below, and saw what she had dreaded.

A gleaming black and silver Harley-Davidson.

The biker was as anonymous and robotic as ever, smoked visor firmly down and hiding any trace of a human expression. When he spoke, his voice was flat and emotionless, and Marcie realised with a shock that it was in some way electronically altered.

'Omega summons you.'

A hint of anger flared in Marcie.

'And what if I don't want to be summoned? I can ring reception any time, and six burly security men will come and get rid of you. Why shouldn't I get you thrown out? Just tell me that.'

'Because you would not risk Omega's displeasure. Omega's displeasure is your pain, Marcie. But his pleasure is your delight. And Omega has such pretty gifts for you.'

The biker put down a black briefcase on Marcie's bed, and clicked it open.

'Omega is very generous, Marcie. See what gifts I have brought you.'

She took a few steps closer to the bed and looked down into the case. For a split second her heart stopped and she drew in her breath, remembering the pictures in the catalogue she had received in

120

the post only the day before. A procession of images filled her head: figures in leather and chains and rubber and shiny PVC; figures of her deepest fantasies brought to life.

Marcie stretched out trembling hands and lifted out the garment inside the case. A playsuit of the finest leather, black and fragrant with newness. She pressed it to her face, breathing in its intoxicating scent.

'Put it on, Marcie, Put it on now. Omega wishes it.'

There could be no thought of refusal. Swiftly she unbuttoned her blouse and slipped off her skirt. Stockings, bra and panties followed. Strange how unabashed she felt, taking off her clothes in front of this stranger; this stranger who had, only a day before, ridden her on the seat of his motorbike. It did not feel as though she was taking off her clothes for a man: no, she was standing naked before a gleaming black automaton.

She picked up the catsuit and examined it more closely. A central zip down the back seemed the only way in. She tugged it down, and slid her feet into the slender leather legs, enclosing her ankles with tiny zips and buckles. Pulling up the catsuit, she slipped in her arms and breasts and turned her back on the faceless biker. The sound of the zipper sliding upwards was like the sound of the key turning in a cell door. And it was also the sound of a mother's goodnight kiss. For her imprisonment was also her security.

'This, now.'

The biker handed her a smaller garment of black leather: a mask, designed to cover the whole head. She pulled it over her head, and drew down the

121

zip. At first it felt incredibly constricting, pressing coldly against her face. She would not be able to breathe! Only the holes for eyes, nose and mouth made it bearable. But then the pleasure of it dawned on her. Like the helmeted biker, she was now safe within her own world of anonymous sex.

She stepped in front of the full-length mirror, and was immediately shocked by what she saw. Not Marcie MacLean. No, not any longer. This was no laughing redhead with a friendly bosom. The figure who stared back at her from the mirror was a nightmare creature, both captive and wardress. Black-masked and sinister, two emerald green eyes gazed out upon a figure totally encased in black leather. With a sudden pang of excitement, Marcie noted the little zips strategically placed over her breasts, and the zip running from her navel and down between her legs. There could be little doubt what pleasures they were intended to facilitate. Perhaps she would enjoy the impending games in her hotel room.

'It is time to go now.'

Marcie wheeled round, heart thumping.

'Go?'

'Omega wishes it, Marcie.'

'But I can't go anywhere, dressed like this!'

The biker held out spike-heeled boots and a second helmet.

'Put them on.'

Hands trembling, Marcie pulled the full-face helmet over her head. At least now the bizarre mask was covered. She rammed her feet into the too-tight boots, and fiddled clumsily with the side-straps. She felt a good six inches taller, and scarcely able to walk. Could she really dare walk out into the street dressed like this?

'Come with me.'

Marcie was surprised to hear the electronic voice now coming from within the helmet. An intercom. Omega though of everything.

To Marcie's anguish, the biker did not lead her down the back stairs, the modest, easy way to the street. He pushed her in front of him, made her walk before him down the broad, sweeping staircase, into the main foyer of the hotel.

Thank God for the helmet, Marcie thought, feeling her face burn under the mask. All eyes were on her, but at least no-one knew who she was. Surely no-one could guess that this leather queen, bedecked in buckles and straps and zips, teetering on spike-heeled boots, was the same woman as the demure red-head in the business suit who had checked in only hours before. And in Berlin, it took a great deal to shock people.

He was behind her, very close behind; not touching, but his presence was all around her, urging her forward. Do not flinch now, it seemed to say. Omega has great hopes for you. Do not let him down. She stumbled on the stairs once, unaccustomed to the ridiculously high heels, and his leather-gloved hand was there instantly, supporting her and fending off disaster. Suddenly she felt safe and proud.

They walked through the swing doors and out onto the pavement. The golden evening light seemed eerie, viewed through the smoky visor; but the heat permeated the leather suit, and little beads of perspiration sprang up on her skin.

The biker lifted the gleaming machine off the

stand and straddled it. No kick-start: the merest touch of a button, and the engine roared into life. Electronic ignition: nothing but the best for Omega. The faceless visor turned towards her:

'Get on.'

Marcie had never been on a motor-bike before. She didn't even know how to get on. Cautiously, she swung a leg over the leather seat and her toes found the foot-rest on the other side. Perched up there, she felt extraordinarily vulnerable with 1100 cc of hungry horsepower, throbbing through her body, shaking it like a rag doll.

'Hold on to me.'

It was the voice of a sensual automaton, and it seemed to be coming, not from the biker in front of her, but from inside her very head. Tentatively, Marcie placed her hands on either side of the biker's waist.

'Hold on tight. Or you might fall.'

Panic made her tighten her grip. The leather was smooth, hard to get a hold on. Finally she managed to hook her fingers into the biker's belt, but she felt desperately unsafe. She wanted to get off.

But it was too late. With a roar of the throttle, the Harley leapt forward, throwing Marcie against the backrest. She clawed at the biker for safety, pressing herself forward against his unyielding body, a helpless piece of flotsam in the slipstream.

They sped through the streets of Berlin, taking the corners almost without slowing down. The fear was exhilarating, and her pulse began to race. It was a little while before she realised that the laughter she could hear in her head was her own.

The throbbing demon between her thighs used its power over her subtly. With each revolution of the engine, a pulse of energy transmitted itself to the hypersensitive flesh between Marcie's thighs, already teased into life by the hard metal line of the zipper, pressing unforgivingly between her sex lips. An involuntary sigh escaped from her lips.

A voice hissed in her ear:

'Dearest little slut. Omega will be pleased with you.'

The biker's voice, little more than a harsh electronic crackle above the roaring of the wind, shook her back to the reality of what she was doing and feeling. A lone woman leather-clad and masked, riding through a city where she knew no-one, with a man whose face she had never seen. And the spice of fear kindled her desire, making her clitoris throb with an insistent pulse, matching the rhythmic hum of the engine, hot and alive between her thighs.

Marcie had never been to Berlin before, but she knew enough to see that they were now entering what had once been the Eastern sector. The buildings were drab and faceless, crowded together in a maze of dingy alleyways, the tenements so close together that it seemed the sun never quite reached the deepest, darkest corners.

As they bumped over cobbled streets, the metal zipper forced its way more firmly still against her clitoris, and the zip-fasteners across her breasts began to rub themselves over her nipples, stiffening them in spite of her fears.

'Almost there, Marcie. Great things are expected of you tonight. Do not fail us. Do not fail Omega.'

Suddenly angry and afraid, Marcie cried out above the rising tide of her desire:

'But who. . . Who is Omega?'

The biker's head half-turned towards her. She felt sure that, beneath the darkened visor, a thin, cruel mouth was smiling.

'Omega is desire, Marcie. Omega is *your* desire.'

Suddenly the engine cut, and they coasted to a halt outside the seediest and most garish nightclub Marcie had ever seen. Red and blue neon signs depicted naked woman in provocative poses, and yellowing photographs outside the entrance showed men and woman dressed in skin-tight leather and rubber. Strong, well-muscled men dressed as executioners, their desire spurting into the mouths of naked 'slave-girls'. Terrifying leather queens: statuesque young women, their heavy breasts encased in skin-tight leather; their whips raised to punish the miserable naked boys kneeling before them. With a shock, Marcie realised how much like these terrifying women she must look.

'We've arrived, Marcie. Do you like it? Get off the bike.'

Marcie dismounted, slowly and unsteadily. She wasn't going inside that club. No way. She looked around her for her best chance of escape. The bike? No, too big for her to handle. She'd never even get it off the stand. She could run, but this tall, muscular biker would be sure to catch up with her. And if she did get away, where would she go? If she went back to the hotel, Omega would be sure to find her.

Omega, it seemed, was everywhere.

'Take off the helmet, and give it to me.'

She pulled the helmet off, and the shame of her leather-masked face emerged into the dingy evening light. To her surprise, not one of the passers-by turned a hair. Of course, they wouldn't. Oddity and weirdness were common currency in this crummy part of town. If she tried to go her own way round here, dressed like this, what would become of her?

She followed the biker across the few feet of pavement, each step leaden and unwilling. She would not go in there; would not cross that grimy, beaded curtain into the seething underworld whose cacophony floated up to her ears from the basement nightclub. She would not.

And yet she wanted to. Wanted to so very much. Her whole body was crying out for her to walk down those steps and enter the world of waking dreams.

'Come with me.'

Silent and trembling, she walked on her spiky heels across the pavement, and through the beaded curtain.

Chapter Seven

*T*he wall of sound hit her as soon as she put her foot on the top step. It was quite dark in the nightclub, but whirling coloured lights cut through the gloom, lighting up the faces and bodies of a myriad chimera.

The patrons of the Club Justine were far more bizarre, far more outrageous, than any of the yellowing publicity photographs had suggested. That tall figure over there, with the mass of platinum hair and the clinging rubber dress: was that really a woman? The harsh lines of the face gave the secret away; but the man dancing with 'her' didn't seem to care. Perhaps he was too high to realise?

The music had a pounding, brutal beat. It seemed to bounce off the walls, the floor, the ceiling; striking the writhing bodies like the crack of a whip, falling again and again on an expanse of naked flesh.

Pretty boys were dancing in cages, suspended

from the ceiling like bats in a dark cavern. Their naked bodies were glistening; sweet oils slicked over their smooth skin. Not a trace of body hair; that would spoil the line of their carefully sculpted muscles. Marcie could not suppress a surge of excitement as she watched them, their firm young flesh quivering slightly as they pranced and gyrated for the special pleasure of their masters and mistresses. They had clearly been chosen for their delightful cocks, which were uniformly large and thick. The music became louder and more frenetic, and Marcie watched in fascination as the flaccid pipes of flesh grew firm and hard, rearing their heads like deadly serpents, about to strike. She wondered if she could tame their fury.

The biker was still there, in front of her; his hand was on her wrist, dragging her on through the teeming mass of dancers. Her foot caught against something soft, and she looked down: two naked girls were lying on the ground, each tonguing the other's clitoris with loving gentleness. Their nipples were stiff and hard, and one had a bright green stone sparkling in her navel.

Sudden hands pawed at her.

'Schlage mich, schlage mich, meine schöne Prinzesse.'

The biker turned to her and shouted above the noise.

'He wants you to beat him, the poor wretch.'

He kicked the wizened old man out of the way; and his victim seem moderately pleased by the pain, for his cock was swollen beneath his leather pants.

'Well, who is to say that he shall not have his heart's desire, before the night is out?'

She shuddered and instinctively moved away, only to fall into other, more insistent hands. Two women were stroking her now, running ivory whip-handles down the line of her breasts and belly. Their faces were ferocious masks of white foundation and brilliant-red lipstick. Just like vampires, thought Marcie. Vampires who want me to bleed only for them, to slake their unnatural hunger.

She turned away from them, stumbling across the dancefloor in a daze, her head reeling in the fumes from incense burners and joints. There was something very illicit in the air, and it was going straight to her head. These people, these monsters of perverse desire, were drugging her, taking away her will. And her treacherous body was crying out a joyous welcome to their world of shameless depravity; laughing its pleasure in the face of unholy, forbidden desires.

Hands reached out, as if from nowhere, and snapped something shut round her throat. Something heavy and rather tight. She put up her own hands to fend it off, and realised what was happening to her. Too late to resist now: the studded leather collar was already about her neck, the symbol of her humility. The biker led her now, not by the arm but by the throat, leading her along on a thick chain, like some placid beast. Her belly was warm with the excitement of it, her head light with the drug in the air.

Two naked men approached, their nipples pierced and little golden chains linking them. Twins! The resemblance was exact, right down to the glorious treasures hanging between their muscular thighs. Their cocks were not shaven like those of the pretty young boys, and Marcie thrilled to see the thick shafts arching up out of dark thickets of curly hair. She reached out and grasped a cock in each hand, immensely enjoying the sensation of hot, hard flesh in her palm. With a few strokes of her wrist, she knew she could make them flood her palm with pearly love-juice. Or what if she took these two men together, one in her mouth and one between her aching, yearning thighs? They had strong, near-perfect bodies, slender hips. They would have great stamina. She would have many, many orgasms before they spurted into her.

But Marcie's escort had other plans for her.

'Come, Marcie. There is work for you to do; tasks for you to perform.'

Dragged forward, she came to edge of the dance-floor and saw that she and the biker were standing in front of a door, marked *Privat* in kitsch gothic characters. Without knocking, the biker opened the door and led Marcie inside.

Three men were sitting in the room. Ordinary-looking men in business suits. They looked almost embarrassed to be discovered in the back room of a dingy night-club, paying for private special services they did not dare demand openly. One was middle-aged and balding, the other two quite young and reasonably good-looking. To Marcie, in her present state of sexual excitement, they all looked desirable enough to fuck with, and that was all that mattered.

'Omega has set you this task,' hissed the biker from within the depths of his inhuman perspex mask. 'To satisfy every desire of these three men. They have paid dearly for their pleasure.' He turned to Marcie and wound the metal leash very tight around her throat, almost choking her. 'And you also shall pay dearly, Marcie, should you dare to fail.'

In a moment he was gone, and the door closed behind him, leaving Marcie alone in the seedy back room with three strangers. Strangers with greedy mouths and insistent hands.

On the giant video-wall in the Club Justine, the patrons watched a masked woman in black leather as she began slowly to undress the first of the men, stripping off his jacket, unbuttoning his trousers, taking out his burgeoning prick.

The biker relaxed in the black and silver chair, and slipped off one leather gauntlet. His hand was bronzed and elegant: not the hand of a rough mechanic. His fingers were well-manicured and on one he wore a silver ring which Marcie would have recognised instantly, had she not been fully occupied elsewhere. A ring engraved with a simple symbol of domination and submission.

Through the visor of the helmet he watched the woman grinding the heel of her spiky boot into the naked flesh of the middle-aged businessman. And now the stiletto heel was insinuating itself oh-so-delicately into his arsehole. The film was silent, but the man's mouth was opening and closing. In pain; in ecstasy? Was he begging her to stop, or was he begging her for more? The rebellious, twitching cock provided the answer.

The biker unzipped his leathers and pulled out his prick. It was hot and hard from the ride, and from the contact of Marcie's luscious body against his back. A young woman who did not yet realise the tremendous power of her own sweet flesh. All about him, men and women were writhing in attitudes of ecstasy, their mutual pain also becoming their greatest pleasure.

Thoughtfully, he began to play with his erection, slowly, so as to make the enjoyment last. On the screen, the young woman was arching her back now, her backside towards the camera as she bent forward over a chair. One of the younger businessmen had unzipped the fastener which led from her navel, between her legs, and now she was bending forard with ivory buttocks and sweet pink womanhood exposed to the indomitable eye of the camera. She, of course, had no idea that she was being filmed. But Omega must have evidence of her obedience.

The woman was crying out now, as a hail of slaps rained upon her naked buttocks, marbling them a delightful red and white. Her cries were silent, but there was a look of bliss upon her face. Her tears were all tears of joy. This revelation of the subtleties of pleasure was clearly a valuable one to her. The biker rubbed his shaft a little harder, cradling his balls as he watched, only too aware of the irony of the situation. Despite the studded leather collar about her neck, this young woman was nobody's slave: all those who watched were in thrall to her. For she held their pleasure in the palm of her hand, in the curve of her breast, the fragrant warmth of her sex.

She was an apt pupil. See how she used her own chains to flay the cringing victim as he knelt before her. See how his cock exploded in jets of white spray as she unzipped one perfect breast and thrust it into his hungry mouth. See how she refused her victims the glory of fucking her, and took her own pleasure, there before them in that sleazy room. She was magnificent.

As she slid the dildo into her soft, wet womanhood, and ran delicate and knowing fingers over her clitoris, the faceless biker shuddered and came; white jets of sperm soiling the mirror-smooth surface of his black leathers. Her victory was complete.

Marcie lay in her hotel bed, listening to the sounds of the city awakening to a summer morning. Her mind was full of disturbing, exciting, compelling images. Images of the night.

She could almost have believed it had all been a dream, if it wasn't for the leather catsuit, lying discarded over the back of an armchair. It looked so harmless, so inoffensive in the golden morning sunshine, a poor, deflated thing with no power to harm or to corrupt. Strange, then, that it had taken over her body and led her to perdition.

She recalled the expressions of the men she had pleasured; and their high, thin cries as she martyred their flesh. Their greedy mouths and fingers, grasping for her breasts and for the sweet succour of her womanhood. The evening had begun with her humiliation, and ended with her glory. Never before had she experienced such an overwhelming exultation of power.

And yet, the dark shadows around the edges of her mind frightened and disorientated her. The faceless figure of Omega stalked her dreams and would not let her go. Whatever she did, Omega knew about. Sometimes, she thought he could even see into her thoughts.

A glance at the clock told her she must get up. In an hour's time she would be seeing Herr Niedermayer, and she mustn't keep him waiting, no matter how exhausted she felt.

She was just getting out of the shower when there was a knock on the door. Breakfast! Slipping on a robe, she went to the door and opened it. There was no-one in sight, but on the floor was a breakfast tray replete with coffee and warm rolls, covered with a spotless white napkin. She went back into the room, nudged the door shut with her foot and then placed the tray on the bedside table.

The coffee was steaming hot and she drank down a scalding cupful, black and sweet, before whisking off the napkin.

There, amongst the soft white rolls, lay a videotape. On top of it there was a small folded piece of paper. She picked it up and read it:

GUARD IT WELL. IT IS YOUR GLORY AND YOUR SHAME. SOON, VERY SOON, YOU SHALL MEET OMEGA.

A videotape? But of what? A sudden sickness clutched at Marcie's heart, and she raced over to the VCR. Shoving the tape into the slot, she pressed the play button.

A leader tape gave way to a series of indecipherable coloured lights, moving about aimlessly against a grey background. Marcie hardly needed to see any more. She understood instantly. She wanted to switch off the tape, but instead she just sat paralysed as the grainy images flickered into focus. A tall, slender woman, masked and clad from head to foot in skintight black leather, was caressing the erect penis of a naked man with her sharp fingernails. He was clearly terrified and thrilled by his mistress's savage love.

Horror-stricken, Marcie leapt across the room and jabbed at the stop button. The tape froze at a frame of the leather queen, an erect penis in either hand, laughing as the white spunk spattered over the front of her leather suit and the studded collar about her slender throat.

Marcie climbed the steps and went through the main doors into reception.

'Guten Tag.' Her German was terrible, but she knew she ought to make an effort, though her knees had turned to jelly. The thought of that video film still filled her mind. The receptionist was smiling encouragingly, and she plucked up all her courage. 'Herr Niedermayer, bitte.'

'Mrs MacLean, yes?'

Marcie nodded, relieved not to have to speak German any more. 'I have an appointment with Herr Niedermayer, for ten o'clock.'

'Do please take a seat. I will let him know you are here.'

Five minutes later, the burnished aluminium lift doors slid apart, and a tall young man with a shock of light-brown curls stepped out, his hand extended in greeting.

'Herr Niedermayer?'

'Sebastian Ernst, Herr Niedermayer's personal secretary.' He smiled, no doubt enjoying Marcie's confusion. She blushed, not just because of embarrassment but because this young man really was quite devastatingly beautiful. She looked down and saw that his hands were slender, like a concert pianist's; slender and sensitive, thought Marcie. A lover's hands.

They stepped into the lift together and the doors slid shut. Ernst made polite conversation, but showed no romantic interest in her. She felt a vague pang of disappointment. As the cage moved slowly upwards, Marcie thought back to that suffocatingly hot afternoon, only a few weeks ago, when she had had a very different experience in a lift. The sensations came back to her now: the mingled feelings of helplessness and supreme power; and she looked into the clear brown eyes of Sebastian Ernst, and felt his soul tremble.

Those few short weeks had changed her. She had learned to use the power of her sexuality, to stop being afraid of it and to take from it what gave her pleasure. Last night, in the Club Justine, Marcie had learned what it is to be the vessel and the instrument of sexual power. Her life had truly changed forever.

The lift reached the twelfth floor, and the doors opened onto a gleaming corridor: black and rose-pink marble, lined with alabaster statuettes. Tacky but exclusive. No expense spared, Marcie mused. Herr Niedermayer is well able to invest in Grünwald & Baker. But will he? Have I the skill to persuade him that there's something in it for him?

Ernst ushered her into Niedermayer's inner office, letting go of her hand a little regretfully, thought Marcie. Such a beautiful young man; skin like burnished gold. Truly a golden boy.

She sat down in the leather armchair and waited for the great man to arrive. No doubt he liked to make a grand entrance after keeping his clients waiting for a while. Her mind wandered over silly things. That funny little Lladro statuette of a girl with a pet lamb, in really terrible taste. Just the sort of thing Sonja would love for her kitsch collection. She must ring Sonja when she got home, and tell her all about this weird adventure. Now that she thought about it, the whole decoration of the office was opulent, yet appalling. She wondered how much Herr Niedermayer had paid his interior designer.

The door opened and a tall young man came in. Young, broad-shouldered and blond. Marcie recognised him instantly.

'Good morning, Frau MacLean. I trust my assistant has been taking good care of you?'

For a split second her heart stopped, the blood draining from her face.

'Is something the matter, Frau MacLean? Are you unwell?'

Of course, he wouldn't recognise her. How could he? The last time he had seen her, she had been a masked leather queen, the faceless instrument of his pleasure and his pain.

'I – I'm fine, thank you. Just a touch of sun. I'm very pleased to meet you.'

She wondered if he could see how she was trembling as she laid her briefcase on his desk and flicked open the catch. His grey-green eyes seemed to be boring into the side of her face, tunnelling into her mind and searching out her innermost secrets.

How could he sit there and smile like that, so placid and casual? Only hours before, he had been her naked victim. Marcie shivered slightly as she recalled the sweat glistening on his shoulders and back; the way his mouth had opened in a silent scream as she ground her heel into his firm young flesh. The way his beautiful, slender penis had stiffened with each cruel, delicious caress, so precisely judged. She had not realised she possessed such judgement.

Oh, how he had stretched out his hands to her, beseeching her, clawing at her leather-clad flesh; at the one perfect breast thrusting through the zipper opening in her leather catsuit. But she had not taken mercy on him. To do so would have been to destroy his pleasure. For Herr Niedermayer, captain of industry though he might be, was a born victim through and through. Even now, Marcie ached for the sight of his beautiful prick, yielding up its tribute to the only mistress who truly knew the secret of his desires.

She closed the case and put it down on the floor beside her.

'I've brought all the figures with me,' she began, trying to sound as professional as possible. 'I think you'll agree that Grünwald & Baker represents a sound economic base, with a promising future. If you decide to come in with us on the Warsaw project, I don't think you'll be disappointed. According to my calculations, you can expect an excellent return on your initial investment.'

Her eyes met his and challenged them, insolent and bright; almost daring him to dispute what she had said.

Niedermayer scanned the figures briefly, then put down the papers and sat back in his chair, hands folded.

'Very impressive figures, Frau MacLean. But what is in it for me? Oh, a trifling profit, perhaps. But as you can see, Niedermayer Industries is not short of cash, and I am not really looking to diversify at the present time. You must satisfy me, Frau MacLean, that there would be certain fringe benefits to any involvement in your company's forward planning.'

Puzzled, Marcie stared back at the German entrepreneur, suspicious and yet not sure what she was hearing.

'Fringe benefits, Herr Niedermayer? Perhaps you could be more specific. As you will see from the financial breakdown,' she indicated the bar chart she had run off on her computer the previous day, 'you could expect up to a fifteen per cent greater share of the British market for your own products, as a result of the positive image generated by – '

'No, no, my dear Frau MacLean. I don't think you quite understand.' Niedermayer reached across the desk and touched her arm. The contact was like an electric shock, reminding her of the previous evening, when these roles of supplicant and tormentor had been reversed. 'You see, I am a very thorough and careful businessman; I have been doing my homework. I know a lot about you, Marcie MacLean. I know that you are beautiful, talented, sexual, and highly discreet.'

Which of her enemies at G&B had prepared this trap for her?

'What precisely are you suggesting, Herr Niedermayer?'

'I want you, Marcie MacLean. I want to enjoy your body, and I want also to enjoy the benefits of your not inconsiderable mind. You are in a unique position of trust within Grünwald & Baker. You could abstract certain items of interesting market information, which you would then deliver to me. In person, naturally. As the liaising officer between my firm and your own, you would need to visit me *very* regularly. Does that not appeal to you, Liebchen?'

His hand was on hers now, crawling all over it like some well-fed spider moving in for the kill. She watched his moving fingers for a moment, unable to draw away, then looked him straight in the eye.

'You're suggesting I become your mistress, and spy for you. And in return, you will invest in the Warsaw project?'

'Absolutely correct, my dear. You are such a sweet, intelligent – dare I say compliant? – girl. You see, the sum of money you are asking me to invest is a trifling amount, but the investment would be a heavy one in terms of time and technology. I must be sure that it would be worthwhile, and so I have determined a price which would suit both of us. Think, Marcie MacLean: think how the successful completion of this deal would help your career at Grünwald & Baker. Think how you would enjoy a fulfilling sexual union with me. From what I have heard, your husband and your lover are most accommodating; I am sure they would not object.'

Anger and laughter rose in Marcie's throat at the same time. She didn't know whether to laugh hysterically, or scream. When the words came, they were icy-calm and quiet.

'Herr Niedermayer, might I suggest you consider another element in our negotiations?'

He was looking at her questioningly now, fascination joining with the lust in his grey-green eyes.

His gaze made her tremble, made her want him in spite of herself, but she was angry and she was resolute. She would not play his despicable game.

'I'm sure your wife, your mother and your two younger sisters would be interested to hear about your membership of a certain club in downtown East Berlin. Not to mention your board of directors. One of them is a bishop, I believe. Ah yes: the Club Justine, I think it's called.'

Niedermayer's eyes widened. In surprise, alarm? It was difficult to tell.

Marcie reached into her handbag for the video-tape. Odd, really, how a sixth sense had made her bring it with her. She'd been terrified to let it out of her sight, in case someone at the hotel got their hands on it.

She showed it to Niedermayer, but kept it out of arm's reach. She was pretty sure Omega wasn't stupid enough for this to be the only copy, but she wasn't taking any chances.

'Last night, at the Club Justine, Herr Nieder-mayer. Although you did not know it, your pleasure was of interest to many people beyond that little back room.'

Panic was in the eyes now; the look of a man cornered and threatened.

'Yes, my dear Herr Niedermayer. Others were watching, and taking note.'

'How do I know that this is not some elaborate trick? How do I know that that tape shows what you say it does?'

Marcie got up, walked over to the VCR by the window, and slotted the tape into the machine. She tilted the Venetian blinds a little to cut out some of the sunlight. It was a grainy picture, and she didn't want her victim to miss one single detail of his starring role. She pressed play and stood back, watching Niedermayer's face with faint amusement.

The businessman was slumped in his leather swivel chair, staring ahead of him with a white, shocked face. Marcie did not look at the screen. She could read every move, every incriminating gesture, in Niedermayer's changing expressions.

He looked at Marcie, a steady, penetrating gaze.

'How did you get this?'

A smile crept across Marcie's face, the irony of the situation not escaping her. Here she was, playing the wronged virgin to his vile seducer, and all along he was watching her on that flickering TV screen dragging the pleasure out of his pain-wracked body. He would never know how and why she had become his nemesis.

'Where it comes from isn't important. Where's it going next, might be a better question.'

'Are you threatening me, Frau MacLean?'

'Whatever makes you think that?'

He looked towards the VCR.

'I could easily destroy that tape, you know.'

The bluff came easily.

'Do you really think that's the only copy?'

There was a short silence. The moving figures on the screen acted out their soundless ballet.

'I've underestimated you.' He gazed at her, now with a mixture of respect and regret. 'What do you want?'

'Your support. The money and the technology, as agreed. No strings. You and I both know you won't lose by it. It's a good deal for your company.'

Niedermayer gave a sigh and picked up the contract Marcie pushed across the desk at him.

'Such a pity, my sweet English ice-maiden. Together, we could have done great things. I could have taught you such tricks of pleasure.'

'You may not realise it,' Marcie replied, picking up the signed contract and placing it carefully inside her briefcase along with the precious video-tape. 'But you already did.'

The glorious sensation of her own power flooded her veins, swelled her heart and made her dizzy with desire. For that brief moment, she forgot her fears.

Whatever his reasons, Omega was taking good care of her.

'My God, Marcie, I've misjudged you.'

Greg Baxter's face was a picture of astonishment as he examined the signed contract.

'I guess I owe you an apology. Fancy going for a drink to celebrate?'

'Not a chance,' Marcie replied with a grin, whisking the paper out of his hands and putting it back into her briefcase. 'I'm worn out after all that travelling, and I'm going home for a rest.'

'I could show you my etchings.'

'Dream on, sucker.'

She met up with Sonja in the car park, and they drove back together through the Surrey country-side.

'How's your sex life?'

Sonja giggled.

'Jim's taken to buying all these kinky sex-aids, and guess what? They're quite a turn-on! Last week he took me to this sex shop in the East End, and it was a real eye-opener, I can tell you. It wasn't just grubby old men; there were young women there, too, buying sex toys for themselves and leather gear to dress up their toy-boys! Do you know, we got so steamed up that on the way home we stopped off in the park and did it in the bushes. It was the best sex I've ever had. Until I spotted the guy with the camera, up a tree!'

'Feminism's come a long way,' Marcie observed wryly, taking a sharp right off the bypass and onto the quieter country lanes.

'Anyhow, what about you?' Sonja demanded. 'You look pretty pleased with yourself. How did your trip go?'

'Very well. I got exactly what I wanted. In fact, I got a bit more than I bargained for.'

Sonja's eyes grew round with interest.

'Omega again?'

'With a vengeance, Sonja. Tell me: have you ever been to a leather club, where pretty naked boys in chains submit to a crazy masked woman with a bullwhip? Do you know what it feels like to be that masked woman, to lose all sense of your ordinary, sane identity and to know the darkness at the heart of all pleasure?

'Sonja, this must sound crazy, but I don't think I can give it up, not now. I know I have to break out of it, but it's like an addiction. The more extreme his demands on me, the more exciting it is. I just don't seem to have the will. The truth is, I'm excited but I'm scared, Sonja. Really scared. What's going to become of me?'

As she reversed into the drive and parked the car outside the cottage, she knew in her heart of hearts that it would not just be Richard who was waiting for her inside. In her mind's eye, she could already see the message flickering on the computer screen:

OMEGA HAS CHOSEN YOU, MARCIE. OMEGA WILL NEVER LET YOU GO.

Dinner with the Colonel and his wife passed uneventfully, and Richard and Marcie tumbled into bed around one o'clock, half drunk and ready for play. For once, Richard's mind seemed entirely on her. Perhaps it was the drink. He slid his hand onto her thigh and it felt almost as good as when they had been courting, all those years ago.

His skin was still fragrant and moist from the shower, as soft as a baby's; and Marcie ran her delighted tongue over shoulders and torso, drinking in his fragrance; his desire, warm and lazy as a lizard uncoiling in the Mediterranean sun. It was a sultry night, and all the windows were open. Outside, Marcie could hear the sounds of night-creatures, calling across the sun-dried fields. They too were seeking pleasure in the darkness.

Soft, sweet pleasure, with no hint of shadows. If there was a darkness, it was the delicious darkness of velvet, the sweet darkness of rich, smooth chocolate. Marcie ran the very tip of her fingernail over Richard's willing flesh, down the length of his flank, and felt his delighted response vibrate through her whole body. He was so hungry for her.

Running her tongue down his cool, firm belly, she thought how like a statue he seemed in the pallid moonlight filtering through the open shutters. A beautiful statue, brought to life by her indulgent kisses.

Marcie's fingers followed her tongue, exploring the hollows and rolling curves of Richard's body; awakening desire in every nerve-ending, brushing lightly over the downy hairs on his belly and flanks, until every one of them strained for a deeper, more lascivious caress.

His arms gripped her suddenly, clasping her in a ferocious embrace that threatened to crush the life out of her.

'Oh God, Marcie. I want you so much. Let me fuck you; fuck you now!'

'No, Richard; don't hurry it. Let me give you more pleasure.'

She was determined not to let him spoil it with his impetuous hunger. He wanted her. Well, fine. Let him want her more, and more still, before at last she granted him the mercy of an orgasm. She would show him what it meant to feel desire. Too often, he had thought only of his own satisfaction.

Tenderly yet urgently she kissed his face: his eyes, his ears, his cheeks; his mouth, which yielded like a flower to her probing tongue. Inside, his mouth was a hot, wet cavern; his tongue, a fluttering, fragile creature, prey to her overwhelming desires.

She was on top of him now, her pelvis grinding against his, pressed hard up against the swelling shaft of his penis. A little patch of cool dampness on her belly told Marcie that Richard's desire was reaching fever-pitch. His breathing was shallow, hurried; and there were little sobs in his voice, almost inaudible yet so very eloquent.

'My love,' she whispered into the nape of his neck. 'Do you truly desire me?'

He groaned, and clutched her to him, desperate for her to part her thighs and let him into the warm wetness of her haven. But she would not. Not yet.

'Want you, want you so much.'

She silenced him with passionate kisses, whilst with her knowing hands she teased and stroked his yearning flesh. She ran her fingers down his flanks, across his chest, and down towards his straining cock, never quite touching it. Then, sliding down his body, she began to lick around the base of his belly; his thighs, his navel, his flanks, the little curls at the extreme base of his heavy balls.

The electric touch of her tongue on his scrotum made him gasp with frustration, and he thrust forward his belly in a vain attempt to make her suck him. He grabbed at her buttocks, tried to slide a hand between their bodies and into the secret cleft between her thighs; but she forced him away from her pleasure-centre. Tonight, she was stronger than him, stronger than both of them, endowed with an unearthly power. Tonight, her pleasure would be hers, and hers alone.

In a sudden movement, she took one of his balls into her mouth, very gently and completely; and began rolling her tongue around it as though it were some delicious sweetmeat.

Poor Richard went wild with frustration, clutching at Marcie's back in frantic lust. But she did not relent, not for one second. The fingers of her left hand fastened about his other bollock and began tormenting it unmercifully, squeezing just hard enough to cause the most agreeable blend of pleasure and discomfort mingled with fear. For the first time in his complacent life, Richard was beginning to glimpse his vulnerability, the degree of trust which he must vest in Marcie as the price for his satisfaction.

Marcie's clitoris was throbbing with a satanic heat; taking over her body, so that it seemed her whole being was pulsating with an invisible, fiendish life.

Desire was taking her over. She was becoming her desire, and nothing more.

She slid back up Richard's body, and straddled his face. He could not see her clearly, but she knew that his whole being must be filled with the heady scent of her aroused womanhood, only inches from her face.

Her hand slid slowly between her thighs, and parted the fragrant lips of her yearning sex. Within, her clitoris glistened like a perfect pearl, kissed by the cool moonlight.

'Feel how I am taking my pleasure, Richard. Feel how the pleasure is all mine.'

The sudden contact of index finger and clitoris surprised even Marcie in its intensity, and her legs almost buckled under the weight of sudden pleasure. The secret flower of her womanhood was flooded with nectar, oozing from between the fleshy petals to form fragrant dewdrops on her deep auburn curls.

Now was the time. Rubbing her clitoris with brutal accuracy, she brought herself to a crashing orgasm which made her cry out with the savage joy of it. And the nectar of her delight trickled forth and formed a fine rain upon her lover's wondering face.

And when she had slaked her desire, slaked it with her own fingers, she straddled her husband's body and admitted his hard urgency to her inner temple, rejoicing in his cries as the agony of pleasure overwhelmed him.

And she would have her victory yet. Riding him skilfully, slowly, with infinite control, Marcie reached out for the bedside table and slid open the drawer. Inside, two silver shapes gleamed in recognition as the moonlight kissed them.

She took them out and, in a single movement, fastened the silver clips onto Richard's nipples.

His cry was a perfect harmony of delight and distress: a sacred agony of pleasure.

And Marcie kissed the pain from Richard's lips; and knew that Omega would not be displeased.

The computer jolted into life with a click and a beep, casting an eerie green light across the sleeping office.

Slowly and silently, a message began to appear on the screen.

Chapter Eight

Marcie yawned, and wriggled her feet into her slippers. She felt tired, jaded, and bored.

Richard had gone, of course. Again. Left in the early hours without even saying goodbye, got into his new red sports car and roared off towards London to do some money-spinning deal that turned him on more than she did. A wave of irritation swept over her. He hardly ever seemed to be around these days.

Well, if Richard couldn't be bothered to spend time with her, she'd find someone who could.

She took coffee and a croissant into the lounge, and worked for a while on a pile of correspondence. It looked very much as if Niedermayer was going to honour his part of the bargain. Two technicians had already arrived from the Hamburg works, and more had been promised by the end of next week.

Jayne Robertson was, of course, incensed. She didn't say anything, but you could see the resentment in her eyes. Marcie, the rookie management consultant Jayne had taken on because she had been ordered to, was getting noticed, and she wasn't. All the previous day at Grünwald & Baker, Marcie had felt Jayne's eyes boring into the back of her head. If looks could kill . . . The irony was that Marcie wasn't the slightest bit interested in her precious Jeremy Stanhope-Miles.

Some of the managers seemed genuinely pleased for her; others gave their congratulations through clenched teeth and fixed smiles. Well, she didn't set out to threaten them, but if they insisted on behaving like spoilt little boys, she wasn't going to lie down and play the good little girlie for them. Oh no: she was going to take her success, like her pleasure, wherever she found it.

Time to type some letters and run off a printout of the latest financial projections. She wondered how the guys would take it when she told them two more senior management posts were going to have to go.

With a shiver, she recalled their phoney smiles, the lust and anger in their eyes; and knew that any one of them might be Omega.

She went into the office and saw it instantly: the flicker of green light on the computer screen.

But the computer had been switched off last night, when she went to bed. Hadn't it? She stepped forward and saw the words snaking across the screen, demanding that she read them, enter once more into the game. She stopped in her tracks, in an agony of indecision.

Outside the window, the summer morning was a riot of birdsong and blossom. Fat bumblebees droned through the hollyhocks, and a sleek white cat lay sleeping in the dappled shade of a climbing rose. Sweet perfume rose from the sun-warmed bushes, and the golden sunlight seemed to enter her flesh, her bones, her veins; challenging the twilight world whose gateway was the flickering computer screen.

It was a clearcut choice: the sunlight or the darkness. Which should she choose? Should she embrace the sunlit warmth of a flower-filled garden, or yield to the far subtler, more insidious temptation of the shadows?

Turning her head away, Marcie reached behind the VDU and flicked the on-off switch. She could turn back. She did not have to play the game, just because Omega wished it. This was her life, her choice. Her pleasure. When she turned the machine back on, the message had disappeared.

She breathed a sigh of relief, and sat down to finish the correspondence. Half an hour, and she would be finished: nothing else urgent to do all day. A whole, beautiful, radiant summer's day and she was all alone, with nothing before her.

She reached for the telephone and dialled Sonja.

'Hi, Marcie! How you doing?'

'Fine, but I'm a little bored. Fancy lunch in town and a stroll along the river?'

'Love to, Marcie, but I'm working this afternoon. Didn't I tell you? Your friend Greg Baxter rang me up the other day, and said he needed a temporary office manager and you'd recommended me to him. That was really nice of you, you know! I mean, let's face it: I'm barely qualified for the job.'

Yeah, really nice, Marcie mused. Except Greg Baxter never even mentioned you to me.

'Anyhow,' Sonja went on, 'I'll see you Saturday. Or next Monday, at work!'

A little click, and the line went dead. Something was going on; Marcie could feel it in her blood. Something big, mysterious, maybe scandalous. Perhaps she should have read that message from Omega, after all.

She shook off the doubts and picked up the receiver again. Alex would drive the dark shadows away. He'd take her in his big bear's arms and hug her to him, and she'd melt away like April snow before the fierce warmth of his desire.

Marcie glanced at her watch. 9.15. Even Alex should be awake by now. Maybe she could catch him before he set off for the office. Lazy bastard. She dialled and waited.

'Hello?'

'Alex. It's Marcie. Are you busy today?'

He laughed.

'That depends on what you've got planned for me, Marcie.'

'I've got to get away, Alex. Just for one day. We could drive out into the country, and have a picnic, like we used to do when we were college kids. It's a beautiful day, and I'm so hot for you. I need to lie with you in the sunshine, feel your hands running over my body, lose myself in pleasure.'

'I want you too, Marcie. If you were here with me, you'd see that it's true. Just thinking about making love with you makes me hard. I want to feel your lips sliding over my cock, feel myself exploding into your mouth.'

'Will you come with me? I can't bear to be alone, not on a day like this.'

'I'll be waiting for you, Marcie.'

* * *

Marcie drove off down the bypass, accelerating into the morning sunshine. Already it was a warm day, and with the hood down on the old MG she felt like she was a kid again. No worries, no responsibilities, nothing to think about except what to do with the rest of this endless summer holiday.

She turned on the radio, and began singing along to the insistent beat of a rock standard, tapping fingers on the dashboard as she swung off onto the B road which led towards Hampton Lacey.

The tune changed, and she hummed along happily. Slow down, you're moving too fast, got to make the morning last.

Feelin' groovy.

Yes, she was feeling pretty good this fine August morning. And looking good, too. She glanced in the mirror and saw a confident, immaculate face smile back at her: sleek red-gold hair, twisted up into a loose knot with an emerald bow. Subtle make-up and glossy lips, set off by a pair of small but expensive clip-on diamond earrings she'd once bought herself as a treat but had never dared wear in case she lost one.

Choosing what to wear hadn't been easy. How to achieve that casual, country look, without losing the sexual advantage? In the end, she'd settled for a simple silk vest and short cotton skirt: casual yet soigné, or at least that was what she hoped. Underneath, a simple body in écru satin, embroidered with blush-pink silk.

The green of the trees had never looked brighter, more vibrant. A light shower around dawn seemed to have washed away all the dust of high summer, and the countryside no longer looked tired and shabby. Tiny, wispy white clouds streaked a clear, pure sky, blue as a blackbird's egg. Nothing bad could happen on a day like this. Sonja's new job at Grünwald & Baker was a pure coincidence, and Omega was nothing more than an adolescent prank, which she'd get to the bottom of sooner or later.

Her whole body seemed to vibrate with life and excitement. The beat of her heart was the pulse of sex. She needed to reaffirm her love of life, needed to reach out and grasp the light. How she needed to feel her naked flesh against Alex's, feel the living warmth of his body enter her and make her whole again.

She had tasted the darkness, and knew its seductive power; but she would not be over-whelmed by it, would not be tempted to embrace it and lose herself in the shadows. Omega might have plans for her, but she was sure as hell not going along with them.

Sure as hell.

Almost there, now. A right turn into a sun-dappled country lane, speeding along under the canopy of over-arching branches. Right again, and she saw him: a tall, friendly, smiling figure in crisp white shirt and flannels, his blond hair and beard glossy in the morning sunshine. Standing there outside the village pub, beatific and open-armed, he seemed the angel of light, the perfect antidote to darkness.

She stopped at the kerb and he hopped in beside her, not bothering to open the door.

'Missed you, darling.'

His strong arms wrapped themselves around

her, urgent hands feeling for the softness of her breasts. She was glad she'd dressed up a little for him. A glance at Alex's crotch was enough to reveal his hunger for her. Yes, dressing up had been exciting but undressing would be even more fun.

As they drove off along the lane, Alex slid his hand across, onto Marcie's thigh.

'Want me, sweetheart?'

His voice was husky with sex.

'Alex – no! You'll make me crash! Let me park the car, it'll be safer.'

But Alex was inexorable and undaunted. His fingers were climbing up her thigh now, insinuating themselves under the hem of her tight, short skirt.

'Keep driving, Marcie. Relax and just let me give you pleasure. Don't fight it. You know how good it will be.'

Struggling desperately to remain calm and concentrate on the road, she gripped the steering wheel and stared straight ahead.

The sensations washed over her, like warm tropical waters on some far-off shore. Desire lapped at the edges of her mind, tensing her fingers on the wheel. Let go, and she might drown, drown forever in these sunlit waters.

Alex was tugging up her skirt now, and yes, she was wriggling, lifting her buttocks, first one and then the other, so that he could hitch the fabric up around her hips. She felt so exposed, so shameless, sitting there with her skirt round her waist, baring the secret triangle between her thighs to the warming sun. The silky stretch fabric was pulled taut across her pubis, denying her lover entry; but he was skilful and determined.

She felt his fingers tremble as they found the three little pearl buttons which held the gusset together. One by one he released them, and as the final button yielded, the silky fabric slid back, baring her russet pubic curls.

She gasped, one hand slipping from the wheel and clamping itself on his.

'No, no, Alex. You can't. Not here!'

'Drive on, Marcie. It's OK, just trust me. You won't come to any harm, I promise you.'

His fingers were warm and determined, and her womanhood responsive, the pleasure-centre of her being giving itself up joyfully to this bold seduction. A voice, very far away, was moaning gently, and Marcie realised with a strange detachment that it was her own. She was driving like an automaton now, almost a part of the car, responding mechanically to the road signs and the occasional cars that passed them on the winding country lane. The danger of the situation was still in her mind, but very far away now, a phantom she could only just glimpse out of the corner of her eye.

Fingers probed her softest, most intimate parts, and Marcie began to tremble, unable to control the onrush of overwhelming pleasure. Her clitoris felt immense, rampantly alive, the pleasure centre to which she was an insignificant adjunct. Pleasure was everything now, and she knew she must surrender to it.

Her pulse quickened as they swung round a bend in the lane, narrowly missing a tractor pulling a rickety old farmcart stacked high with hay. Alex's fingers were massaging her clitoris gently but firmly, and her cunt was oozing an abundance of honey-dew. She tried to close her thighs, exclude him from her inner temple, but she had no will to resist the force of his desire.

Helpless and overwhelmed by sensations, Marcie fell forward onto the wheel, her sex spasming in a series of powerful contractions.

Calmly and without a trace of alarm, Alex leant across and took the wheel, guiding the MG into a layby and putting on the handbrake.

It was a long time before Marcie returned to her senses, blinking in the sunshine as though she had been a long time underground, in sepulchral darkness.

'Are we safe?'

Alex laughed, a good-natured sound accompanied by a broad smile.

'Didn't I promise no harm would come to you?'

Marcie nodded, still shocked.

'And wasn't it good? Didn't it feel nice to come with my fingers on your clitty?'

'It was wonderful. I've never felt anything quite like it.'

She looked at him, crestfallen, and burst out laughing.

'Honestly, Alex, just for a moment I thought you were trying to kill us both! But it was great, it really was. In fact . . .'

'What?'

'It was so good, I'm ready to start all over again!'

They drove on for a couple more miles, until they reached a lush, rolling hillside half-covered with mature trees. Marcie cut the engine and let the car coast to a standstill on the dry, sun-

161

bleached grass. Underneath the trees, the grass looked much softer, lush and green. And it was so quiet: nothing but the skylarks and the swifts to disturb their private pleasure.

'Here looks as good as anywhere,' Marcie remarked, skipping out of the car and pulling the picnic basket out of the boot.

Alex clambered out, stretching his long legs and yawning.

'God, I'm tired,' he announced, with a twinkle in his eye. 'I think I need a lie down. How about you?'

'Oh, absolutely exhausted!'

They made their way up the hillside like the two giggly students they had been not so many years before. Above them, the tall trees swayed in the gentle breeze, filling the air with the hypnotic swish of branches; and the whirring of crickets in the long grass formed a dizzy, monotonous counterpoint.

They kissed passionately in the green shadows, hands exploring each other's bodies urgently, yet knowingly. They understood each other's needs, each other's joys and desires, as instinctively as if they had been lovers in some previous life. Perhaps they had.

Marcie's hands slid down towards Alex's burgeoning erection. Excited almost beyond endurance by the episode in the car, his poor frustrated prick was straining against the fabric of his pale grey linen trousers. Just a tiny amount of dampness had leaked through onto the spotless fabric. Hurriedly, she fumbled for the zipper and tugged it down, thrusting in eager fingers to worship his hardness.

Still giggling, they tumbled down onto the soft, springy bracken and Marcie rolled obligingly onto her back, to let him in. She wanted no niceties, not now, no elaborate foreplay or romantic gestures. All she wanted was to be fucked: here, now, without delay.

He was hot and hard, more than ready for her. His thrusts drove against her womb, and she spread her thighs ever wider, anxious to take him further and further into her. Her clitoris sparked into incandescent life, and she began to cry out; wordless syllables of nonsense, the logic of passion. Sweat trickled down the moist crevice between her breasts. Alex's mouth was crushed against hers, his tongue possessing her as his cock was, summarily and without demur.

Coming up for air, he nuzzled into her neck, and Marcie heard his voice, breathless and urgent in her ear:

'Only for you, Marcie. Only ever for you.'

She answered his passion with thrusts of her hips; and they rode the swell of passion together towards its glittering summit.

With a cry of deliverance, Marcie's whole being exploded into a dazzling diorama of coloured lights and sweet, sweet pleasure.

Afterwards, they lay together for a little while, listening to the gentle harmony of their breathing. Then Marcie sat up and stretched.

'Fancy a glass of champagne?'

She opened the cool-box and took out a bottle of Mumm, still deliciously chilled. The cork shot across the clearing, and the creamy white foam spilled out onto the bracken. They caught most of

163

it in their glasses, and toasted each other in chilled champagne.

Marcie savoured the bitter-sweet taste, the delicious pin-pricks as each of a million tiny bubbles burst on her greedy tongue. She felt intoxicated already. Not by the alcohol, but the day: seething with life, below, above, all around her. Birdsong and the song of the crickets; the very earth beneath her seemed to pulsate with its own rich, teeming life.

She giggled to herself, suddenly thinking of a diverting idea. There was a pot of clotted cream in the picnic basket. What pretty games they could play with it. Rolling over onto her belly, she pulled the picnic basket towards her and opened the lid.

There, on top of the food she had packed, was a sizeable box which she most certainly hadn't.

Marcie glanced across at her lover. Alex was resting against a tree trunk, his eyes closed in contented contemplation of the wine. With bated breath, she read the message on the lid of the box: *YOU CANNOT DENY THE WILL OF OMEGA, MARCIE. OMEGA ALONE IS THE SOURCE OF TRUE FULFILMENT*

How could it have got into the basket? Alex? No, of course not. The basket had been in the boot all along, there was no way he could have interfered with it. Breathless, she took the lid off the box. Inside lay a bizarre collection of objects: handcuffs, plaited silken rope, leather thongs, a scourge, and a pair of black leather gloves, one with a palm of the softest fur, and the other covered in metal spikes, wickedly sharp and gleaming.

Marcie's mind was a turmoil of conflicting

desires. She wanted to fuck; yes, fuck in the golden summer sunlight. But she wanted also to enjoy another, far subtler pleasure. A pleasure which Omega had seen written on her heart, and had miraculously provided for. A sinister, remembered phrase kept repeating itself in her head:

Do what thou wilt shall be the whole of the law.

Silently she slipped on the gloves, quivering with the pleasure of the supple leather against her tanned skin. Then she picked up a length of silken cord, and walked towards Alex.

He opened her eyes at her approach, and smiled.

'Little games, Marcie? You want me to tie you up? How intriguing!'

Her heartbeat quickened. He could see only the supple, shiny backs of the leather gauntlets; he could have no idea of the strange gifts they contained within the closed palms. She would keep him guessing.

'Won't you get undressed for me, darling?'

She realised that her voice was unusually deep and husky, as though she had imbibed the pure elixir of sex along with the champagne. How could a few sips of champagne be so powerful? She thought back to that night in the Club Justine, and how her head had reeled as she took part in the orgy with Niedermayer and his companions. Had she again been drugged in some way?

Alex had guessed nothing. Already he had kicked off his shoes, and was peeling off his shirt and trousers, to reveal the skimpiest of black g-strings underneath: a shiny black garment in stretch fabric, which revealed far more than it concealed. Golden pubic curls were escaping from underneath the taut fabric, and his penis was clearly outlined underneath.

Marcie reached out and pulled down the g-string. Alex obligingly finished the job, stepping out of the tiny garment and throwing it onto the ground.

'Well I'm ready,' he announced with a grin. 'Now, how about you, my sweet little darling?'

Marcie neatly sidestepped his clutching hands.

'No, no. First, I want to give *you* pleasure,' she said. 'Lie down, and let me love you.'

In mock obedience, Alex stretched out on the soft grass. His body was as beautiful and still as sculpted stone, polished to the finest sheen.

Marcie went to work quickly, binding his wrists with the silken cord and attaching it in turn to the tree trunk. Now he was her prisoner, utterly at her mercy.

Alex's eyes shot open, the first hint of unease in that confident gaze.

'Hey, Marcie, what the heck are you up to?'

'It's just my way of loving you. Trust me, relax: I know you're going to enjoy it.'

'But I'm not into this bondage crap. And I never thought you were, either.'

With a grim smile, Marcie recollected that day, in the cottage garden, when Alex had imposed the ferocity of his own will upon her. He hadn't minded dominating *her*.

'Relax, sweetheart. It's all for your pleasure, I promise.'

He closed his eyes, lay back and surrendered to her gentle ministrations. Only he wasn't really surrendering, of course: it was all just a game to him. She was playing the dominatrix, and he was playing the happy slave, all the time knowing the roles were really reversed. It was a little indulgence he was happy enough to grant his lover. And it was certainly a stimulating novelty.

She began by opening up her right hand, exposing the fur-lined palm; and she ran it softly over Alex's thighs, his belly, his chest, skirting round his most sensitive places, for she wished to relish her power over him, have him begging for her to put an end to his torment.

He gave a delicious groan as she brushed the tip of his penis with the fur-lined glove.

'Oh Marcie, that feels incredible. Bring me off now; bring me off, I'm good and ready.'

Something about his complacency enraged her, filled her belly with a ferocious desire. It was a desire for pleasure, but not the simple pleasure of having Alex's hardness inside her, pumping pleasure into her willing loins. No, this was the subtle pleasure of control. He would thank her for it, would love her all the more for the ingenuity of her lovemaking.

She opened the palm of her left hand, and with her right, she picked up the leather scourge. All was ready now.

'You can open your eyes, Alex. I want you to see what I have in store for your pleasure.'

His beatific smile soon faded as he saw the scourge, raised in the air and about to fall upon his naked flesh; the spiked glove, stealing its way up the inside of his thigh towards his balls.

'My God, Marcie, what the hell are you doing?' He wriggled about in his bonds, trying to free his wrists from the silken cord.

Somehow, she had expected him to join her in

the game, to welcome the pain and pleasure with an equal joy. His cowardice was a revelation to her. A revelation and a deep disappointment.

'What's the matter with you, Marcie? You never used to be like this. You've changed. And I'm not sure I like it.'

She looked down at him, bronzed and magnificient and utterly pathetic, and the desire drained out of her. All his strength seemed to evaporate before her eyes, and all her passion went with it.

Suddenly dispirited, she let the scourge fall to the ground, pulled off the gloves and threw them in disgust onto Alex's naked body.

'Untie me, Marcie. For God's sake stop playing these bloody silly games.'

Turning round, Marcie walked away down the hill, towards the car. Slowly and calmly she got in, turned the key in the ignition and drove off towards the road. She did not look back.

Hanchester was busy. It was market day. Marcie was sitting outside a cafe in the market place, sipping black coffee and watching the world go by.

A good lunch, a glass of wine and a lot of sunshine had gone a long way towards dispelling the bad thoughts, the uncomfortable memories. She wondered now if she ought to go back and see if poor old Alex was all right. Yes, of course he was. The cords had been thin, the knots loose. He'd have wriggled free in a few minutes. The only thing hurting now would be his dignity. Would he ever forgive her? Did she care whether he did or not?

What had come over her in that field? Alex was

right: she had changed, and how! Simple pleasures were no longer enough. In fact, she wasn't even sure that she liked herself very much any more.

Still, what the hell, eh? She was young, alive, sophisticated. And still hungry for sex. Alex had failed to satisfy her, so she would find somebody who could. She was looking good and turning heads in this anonymous provincial town, where she knew nobody and nobody knew her. Here, she could be whoever and whatever she wanted to be. What was to stop her picking up a total stranger, and taking him to a cheap hotel for an afternoon of guilt-free sex? Omega and Richard and Alex could all go hang: she had only one aim in life today, and that was the satisfaction of her own needs.

No-one's pulling my strings, she thought to herself. No-one but Marcie MacLean.

A tall young man with a briefcase sat down opposite her, and they exchanged smiles. He would do. He would do very well. To start off with. He was young enough to be malleable, old enough to have experience.

He was looking at her, and trying to look as if he wasn't. Well, she would make him sit up and take notice of her. She snaked her foot under the table, and made contact with the young man's leg. He started, and looked up at her, searching her face for some sign: was it an accident, or had she meant it?

She removed the uncertainty by repeating the exercise, but this time with greater deliberation. She kicked of her shoe, and let her toes slide playfully up his pinstriped leg. She could almost hear him gulp as he swallowed heavily.

Her toes climbed higher, emboldened by the smile which suddenly illuminated his face. He, at least, understood the game and was willing to go along with it. He shuffled his feet just a little further apart, for her to slide her toes between his thighs. He felt hot and hard against her bare foot, full of youthful impetuosity. A little shiver ran through her as she thought of all the fun they were going to have together, even though he didn't realise it yet.

She was relaxing, enjoying herself. Life was good. She was caressing a stranger with her naked toes, and the warm sun was caressing her like a genial lover.

And then something – a sound, a movement? – made her glance across the square. The bustling crowds around the market stalls confused her for a moment, but there was no mistaking what she had seen.

The black and silver bike was parked on the other side of the square, a snarling mass of gleaming metal amid the Sierras and the four-wheel-drive jeeps. There was no mistaking it. There could not be two bikes like it. It glittered with a ferocity of burnished chrome.

Her head swam. Surely there must be some mistake.

And she looked back across the square, to the spot where the leather-clad biker was standing, blank-faced behind the smoked black visor. He seemed to be waiting for something.

Or someone.

Chapter Nine

'**G**et on the bike.'

The blank face seemed to be staring right through her. What crazy impulse had made her get up from her seat and walk towards him across the market square? Why should she obey him? What could he possibly do to harm her, here in the middle of a busy market town on a sunny afternoon?

Why did she fear him?

She took the proffered helmet and pulled it down over her face, once again entering the stifling twilight world of waking dreams. The intercom clicked on, and the electronic voice hissed in her head:

'Get on. I'm taking you on a little trip.'

She looked into the faceless visor and once again had the eerie impression that she was talking to an automaton, a creature of wires and glass and metal, beneath the taut leather skin which concealed a heart of whirring steel. A sex-robot, ruthless and efficient; the perfect messenger for Omega. Or was this Omega himself?

As though reading her thoughts, the voice entered her head again:

'I am not what you seek, Marcie. I am Omega's messenger, that is all. We must all be ready to serve the will of Omega.'

Sitting astride the Harley, pressed up tight against the rider's back, Marcie stopped wondering what was going to happen to her, and surrendered to the intoxication of speed, the hypnotic succession of images as they raced out of the market square and out onto the main road.

A sign flashed by: *London 25 miles*. So that was where he was taking her. Curiosity flickered through her brain. But her body was already taking up more of her attention. Her skirt was up round her backside, and her bare thighs were pressed up tight against the biker's leathers. The rushing slipstream buffeted her bare arms and legs with rough caresses, deliciously cool in the oppressive summer air; filling her with a wildness she had never felt before.

The bike tilted alarmingly to the right as they went round a sharp bend. Suddenly afraid of falling, Marcie clung onto the rider and squeezed her legs tighter against his smooth, strong thighs. Her breasts were squashed up against his back, and the constant bumping up and down rubbed her nipples – protected only by her thin silk blouse – against the studded leather. She began to breathe heavily, for the contact was by no means unpleasant. The sound was picked up by the microphone in her helmet, and she heard a little dry laugh.

'Desire is your master, Marcie. Shame is a forgotten fear. Omega has chosen well.'

Far from damping down her desire, the biker's words served only to increase Marcie's excitement. She rubbed herself harder against the biker's back, excited by the thought of taking her pleasure entirely as she chose, and in the full glare of the afternoon sunlight.

Between her bare thighs, the shiny leather seat quivered, transmitting vibrations from the powerful engine. 1100 cc of pure, throbbing sex, oiled and gleaming; piston-rods thrusting relentlessly in and out of well-oiled cylinders.

Marcie gasped, her love-lips damp and so, so sensitive against the hot leather. Each throb of the engine seemed to enter her very soul, both soothing and exciting her beyond endurance, its rhythm the rhythm of pure sex.

She came in a juddering spasm of pleasure that racked her whole body, a low moan escaping her lips, despite her attempts at self-restraint. She could not conceal her pleasure. Not from Omega.

'Don't fight it, Marcie. Desire is good. Pleasure is good. Only denial is to be denied.'

Almost sobbing with confusion and fear, Marcie gripped the biker's waist, her knuckles whitening with the tension. Her head was spinning; she scarcely knew who or what she was any more, let alone where.

The rest of the journey passed in a daze; a multi-coloured smear of noise and traffic, speeding past Marcie's eyes on a never-ending conveyor belt. They stopped a few times at traffic lights, wove in and out of the traffic in the centre of town, but Marcie took little interest in what was around her.

She had abandoned herself to the rhythm of Omega's overwhelming will.

'We're here, Marcie. Get off the bike and give me your helmet.'

The bike slid to a halt beside the kerb in a busy city street, and the rider helped Marcie to dismount. Her legs felt stiff and shaky, and he had to help her walk the few steps across the pavement to the office block. It was shiny, new; faceless as all new office blocks are, a Babel of towering glass and polished granite.

They walked in through the automatic doors, and past a reception desk where a security guard nodded respectfully as the biker flashed an ID too quickly for Marcie to see what it read. Oddly enough, she wasn't sure she wanted to see. The thought of knowing brought with it fear. Simply to abandon herself to events, to another, greater will, was also to abandon the fear of knowing. She tried to empty her mind of all thoughts, and followed the biker further into the building.

In the centre of the entrance hall was an elaborate criss-crossing of escalators, some leading down into the basement, others leading upwards in a seemingly endless herringbone towards a dizzying glass dome, many floors above. Workers were going about their business: anonymous, smart-suited figures carrying files and briefcases; but not one of them took any notice of Marcie. The biker ignored the escalators and led Marcie towards the lifts.

She followed him inside, a little shiver of apprehension rippling though her as the doors closed, imprisoning her in an airless cocoon. She could not block out the memory of that other lift; that darkened cage where she had first encountered the dream – or was it a nightmare? – that was Omega.

But the biker showed no sign of intending to lay a finger on her. He seemed as detached, as impersonal, as the faceless outfit he was wearing. Marcie found herself almost wishing he would yield to some obscene desire, give in to some wild impulse and reveal the humanity behind his mask. This calm, this detached, he was far more unnerving than any leering drunkard in a back alley.

At the thirtieth floor, the lift jolted to a halt and the door slid open. Marcie hesitated.

'After you.'

The biker's synthetic voice was heavy with irony. His parody of the perfect gentleman irritated her, frightened her too.

They stepped out onto a gleaming marble floor, immediately beneath the vast glass dome of the building.

'Look down, Marcie.'

Marcie obeyed, clutching the brass rail as vertigo gripped her. She was looking down into the entrails of the building, down through the criss-crossing escalators and into each floor. Dark-suited men and women were working at desks, travelling silently up and down from floor to floor. No-one was speaking. An eerie silence prevailed. It seemed an endless pattern, which vanished into the very depths of the earth. Into the depths of hell.

'Omega built this, Marcie.'

The biker was gripping her arm now, and urging her to turn and look out of the glass wall behind her. She obeyed, and saw a dizzying panorama laid out below her: the multi-coloured maze of a docklands development; the only one, it seemed, still thriving in the midst of economic gloom.

'And this, Marcie. It is all the work of Omega.'

'I don't understand. How can it be?'

'You do not need to understand, Marcie. Only to accept. And to submit.'

They travelled back down in the lift, Marcie's head full of wonders and doubts. Could it possibly be true that Omega's influence stretched this far, into the heart of the City?

As they passed the reception desk and went out again, into the dazzling sunshine, Marcie's eye was caught by something she had not noticed on the way in. A little brass plaque, just beside the entrance. It read: *Grünwald & Baker plc*.

Breathless with shock and with the sudden confirmation of half-realised suspicions, Marcie followed the biker in a daze, put on her helmet and dutifully mounted the bike. They roared off into the afternoon traffic, dodging taxis and pushbike couriers, and heading off towards south-west London. As they sped past the Houses of Parliament, Marcie's heart contracted with fear. For the biker was pointing towards the House of Commons with outstretched hand.

'That is Omega's house, Marcie. All within belongs to Omega.'

They rode on, Marcie not daring to break the silence for fear of hearing more outrageous, unacceptable horrors. Could it really be as the biker had told her? Or was it all an elaborate joke? But her eyes had not deceived her. She had seen the brass plaque. And the security guard had acknowledged them. He had not even questioned her presence there, without an ID.

The bike slowed down as they passed a computer dealer's showroom; the very one which Grünwald and Baker used, Marcie recalled. She remembered going along there with the IT systems manager, a year ago, to pick up her own terminal and take a day's training course.

'Behold: the voice of Omega,' hissed the biker in Marcie's ear. Through the electronic crackle, she realised that there was not a trace of irony in his voice. What was he telling her: that Omega had infiltrated more than just one computer? That Omega was in every office, on every computer screen?

And what was the messenger hiding behind the cloak of anonymity? What other terrible truths would be forced upon her if she could see beyond the darkened visor?

Behind her own visor, Marcie closed her eyes and surrendered to the howling darkness of her fear.

It was an unremarkable building: a two-storey terraced house in a faceless suburb. The front garden was neat and tidy, the paintwork a sensible dove grey. Nothing about the house proclaimed that it was notable in any way.

Nothing but the discreet plaque that read: *Omega Foundation*.

'I'm not going in there,' whispered Marcie as the key turned in the lock and the biker's gloved hand pushed open the front door. The last time was still engraved on her mind: the time when a black and silver card had lured her to a deserted house.

Deserted save for the naked victim, hanging terrified and helpless in a blaze of candlelight. Tears pricked her eyelids as she recalled the newspaper headline: 'Mysterious blaze in derelict house. Arson suspected'. And yet there had been no mention of a body, no mention of a terrible accident.

'You must go in, Marcie. You must confront your fears, or you will never overcome them.'

He had her by the wrist, not tightly, but the grip was an authoritative one. It said: I do not want to harm you; I do not want to force you to go in. But be under no illusion. I can make you do anything I choose. She made to remove her crash helmet, but the biker's hand restrained her.

Reluctantly she stepped into the house, shaking her wrist free of his grip. Immediately she felt a surge of relief. This was no darkened hell-house, all dusty drapes and bare floorboards. The house was brightly decorated with Liberty prints and lush, soft carpets. Nothing remotely unsavoury could ever happen here.

'Up the stairs, Marcie. Go right up to the top, and through the door in front of you. I shall be right behind you.'

She climbed the stairs, admiring the Renoir prints and the little Oriental curios. At the top, she hesitated. A door stood directly in front of her, inoffensive in pink and white eggshell paint; but resolutely closed.

'Go in.'

'I can't.'

'Do it, Marcie.'

She pushed open the door and stepped inside.

The room was painted plain white, almost clini-

cal in its antiseptic gleam, and a stark contrast to
the rest of the house. At the far end of the room
were two chairs, facing a curtained-off section of
wall.

'Sit down, Marcie. I have something to show
you.'

She obeyed a sense of foreboding washing over
her; and the biker pulled a cord, drawing back the
grey curtain.

At first, she could not quite believe what she
was seeing. It didn't make sense, like some crazy,
surrealistic film. Only the figures were so clear, so
close to her. She looked questioningly at the biker,
enigmatic behind his visor.

'It is all real, Marcie. You are looking through
one-way glass. They cannot see you, though you
can see them'.

She turned back to the mirror, her window on
hell. Inside the room next door, two figures were
engaged in a strange and fascinating ritual. It was
all the more chilling for it happened in silence, all
sound blocked off by the intervening wall. A naked
woman, blonde and gaudy in red lipstick and a
bright blue leather mask, was bending forward
over a wooden saw-horse. Her buttocks were
thrust backwards, and were striped with red welts.
The bamboo cane lying on the ground beside her
left Marcie in no doubt as to how she had come to
be in this state.

About the woman's neck was a studded leather
collar, and instinctively Marcie raised her hand to
her own throat, half-expecting to feel the mark of
her own subjugation. Two chains extended from
the woman's collar to two leather wrist-bands,

which were in turn chained to a leather belt around her waist.

Her wrists were chained to the saw-horse, and she was clearly helpless, yet she was laughing; laughing almost manically, thought Marcie. The masked man behind her was clad in a black leather harness which encased most of his torso but left his buttocks and thighs exposed. Marcie wished that he would turn and face her, so that she could see his dancing prick.

As she watched, he approached the woman and Marcie caught sight of his hardness, the upward soaring curve of his cock strangely familiar, strangely reassuring. He prised open the woman's glistening red lips and thrust into her, at the same time bringing down the cane upon her arching back. She tensed at the blow, but seemed still to be smiling, even as the masked man thrust into her.

'What has all this to do with me?'

'Patience, Marcie. All shall be made clear.'

The masked man was thrusting harder and faster now, his buttocks tensing and untensing as his prick entered the woman's mouth. There was pleasure on her face; ecstasy, even. Marcie found her own excitement mounting as she looked at the woman's breasts quivering with each thrust.

And he came into her, shuddering with pleasure; mouth opened in a soundless acclamation of his joy.

He pulled off the woman's mask to kiss her closed eyes, and Marcie leapt to her feet in amazement. Jayne Robertson! Jayne Robertson in a mask and chains.

The man was laughing now; laughing and reaching up to his face, unlacing the leather mask which enclosed his face. Still laughing, he emerged into the cruel white light, shaking his golden locks with merriment.

The biker was looking at her now. Though she could not see his face, she knew his eyes were boring into her, searching her soul, trying to drink in the depth of her shock, her revulsion.

The weird, electronic voice spoke in her head once again. She shook her head, closed her eyes, but it refused to be silent.

'Listen to me. Listen to me, Marcie. Yield to Omega. Yield now.'

'Never!'

'Yield to Omega, Marcie. Your only loyalty is to your pleasure.'

'I . . . I can't.'

The biker's gloved hands were on her body, stroking her, stimulating her, pressing her against him. She could feel his readiness for her, throbbing through the tight leather as he thrust against her belly. He wanted her; and in spite of herself, in spite of the weird scene she had just witnessed, she wanted him to. Yield to Omega; yield to pleasure. The biker's touch felt delicious upon her bare skin, his gloved hands pulling up her blouse, feeling the warm, naked flesh beneath.

The electronic hiss filled her mind, her body, her soul.

'Omega loves you, Marcie. Only Omega.'

His gauntleted fingers touched her nipple and it felt like an electric shock, bringing her back to reality. She was no sex-toy, no slave; she was Marcie MacLean, and she would not yield to the nightmare world of her own fantasies. No: she was stronger than that.

'Let go of me!'

She drew away, catching the biker by surprise. He made no attempt to stop her as she wrenched open the door and half-ran, half-flung herself down the stairs to the front door, pulling the black helmet from her head and dropping it on the hall carpet.

Outside, on the pavement, she glanced back for a moment through the open front door. There was no sign of the biker. The Liberty prints smiled back at her like the obscene leer of a clown, depraved beneath a veneer of innocent fun.

She ran down the avenue to the main road, where she hailed a taxi.

'Waterloo Station.'

As the taxi sped away, she turned and looked back at the house receding into the far distance. Somewhere at the back of her mind, she thought she heard the sound of distant laughter.

It wasn't until she got off the train, tired and shaken, that Marcie remembered the car. She'd left the MG parked in the market square at Hanchester! God only knows what'll have happened to it by now, she thought to herself, walking down the village street towards the cottage. Right now, she didn't much care.

'Good evening, Mrs MacLean.'

She nodded her acknowledgement to the Colonel's wife, not wishing to get involved in a conversation right now.

'Did you have a nice picnic?'

'Er – yes, thanks.'

Marcie watched in amazement as the Colonel's wife went into the Old Rectory with her shopping basket. She knew the old bat was nosey, but how had she found out about the picnic? Marcie hadn't told a soul.

As she walked up the private road to the cottage, she stopped dead in her tracks. There, in front of the house, was the MG! She ran towards it and found it was completely unharmed, and maybe even a little cleaner.

The keys were in the ignition, and there was an envelope on the front seat. Beside it, a single blood-red rose. Nervously, she tore open the envelope.

It contained a plain black card, with a simple silver symbol.

Omega. Nothing more. No message to taunt or excite her.

Wearily, she went into the cottage. Richard wasn't back yet. No messages on the answerphone, so nothing from Alex. Alex! Was it any wonder he hadn't called?

And now this revelation about Jayne Robertson. How long had she been involved with Omega? And what had it all got to do with Grünwald & Baker? She sank into a chair and put her head in her hands.

A thought hit her. Life must go on. Got to enter those figures onto the computer for the meeting on Tuesday. She made herself a strong black coffee, and sat down at her desk.

Enter the password: *JUNO*.

INCORRECT PASSWORD.

She was tired. She must have entered it wrongly. She tried again: *JUNO*.

INCORRECT PASSWORD. ACCESS DENIED.
JUNO. JUNO.
ACCESS DENIED. PASSWORD HAS BEEN
CHANGED.

The system was shutting her out! What the hell was happening? Who could have changed her password?

She was about to pick up the phone to call the engineer when it rang.

'Hello?'

'Marcie, darling, it's Richard. I've been trying you all day.'

A wave of gratitude flooded her and she almost burst into tears.

'Oh, Richard, I've missed you. I was out. I'm sorry.'

'No problem, sweetheart. Listen, I'm sorry but I can't get home to you tonight. Sir Tony is keeping us working all evening, and I've booked myself into a hotel for the night. But look; I feel I've been neglecting you, I really do. What do you say to a day out tomorrow?'

'That would be lovely. Where shall we go?'

'Well, I've got a little surprise for you, Marcie. There's something I'd really like to show you. Will you meet me tomorrow morning, in Soho?'

'Soho! Why?'

'A friend of mine has a company which has just opened a new outlet there. It's a really wonderful shop selling sexy underwear, playsuits, you know the sort of thing. Good, harmless fun. It's called "Mistress Mine" and it's in a little lane not far from Wardour Street. Will you meet me there? I thought maybe we could buy each other some fun clothes, maybe one or two little sex toys; then go off for an aphrodisiac lunch and spend the afternoon in a five-star hotel. What do you say?'

Marcie laughed.

'It's not like you to be so adventurous.'

'I've had a change of heart, Marcie; really I have. Say you'll come.'

'OK, Richard. It's a date.'

'Ten o'clock outside the shop?'

'See you there. Sweet dreams, darling.'

The receiver clicked back into place, and Marcie was alone again with an unco-operative computer.

A sudden thought hit her; and with trembling fingers she entered in the letters.

NEW PASSWORD: OMEGA.

A few seconds passed, and she thought she had been mistaken. Then the screen cleared.

PASSWORD OMEGA. WELCOME TO THE NETWORK, MARCIE. OMEGA WELCOMES YOU.

Chapter Ten

Marcie stood outside the shop, darting glances to left and right. Had anyone noticed her standing there? Should she leave; or dare she go inside?

Richard's 'little adventure' had seemed like a good idea the night before. Now, she wasn't so sure. As she stood outside Mistress Mine in the unforgiving morning light, nerves clutched at her stomach. This wasn't how she'd expected it to be. Richard had implied that it would be a harmless little playwear shop: a place where you could have a giggle, buy a few sexy undies. But this was something else; something infinitely darker, which stirred depths in her that she longed to deny. But she knew she could not.

Still, rightly or wrongly, she was here, staring wonderingly into the garish window of a fetish-wear shop in a downtown backstreet; and strange feelings were stirring inside her. She couldn't help thinking back to what had happened that night in the Club Justine; to a slender figure in black leather and spike-heeled boots, laughing behind her mask because all power was hers: because she was the mistress of divine agony.

Worst of all on this nerve-wracking morning, Richard was late. Marcie glanced at her watch. Ten-thirty already, and still no sign of him. Maybe he'd been delayed by some urgent business call. It wouldn't be the first time that he'd put business before pleasure, she mused with a tinge of bitterness.

Maybe she should simply leave, and teach him a lesson. Walk away, and find something better to do with her time. Why should she be at his beck and call, or at any man's beck and call for that matter; ready to drop whatever she was doing whenever he had a spare moment for her? She wasn't beholden to him. Whatever she had in life, she had gained for herself, by herself. No favours. No lucky breaks.

No Omega.

Remorse pricked her conscience. When all was said and done, Richard might be boring but he wasn't deceitful. She thought of what she had seen in that weird terraced house, only the previous afternoon. Jayne Robertson as she had never seen or even imagined her before. And she shivered, suddenly afraid.

Should she try to telephone Richard? But there was no phone nearby, and if he arrived to find she wasn't there, maybe he'd assume she'd chickened out. No; she'd promised to be there, and she would see it through. The idea of an adventure intrigued her.

One thing was for sure: this wasn't a very

salubrious area, even in the middle of an August morning. Not the sort of place you'd expect to find a young woman, alone. This was the sort of district where the sun never quite dispelled the shadows, even at midsummer noon. The street was scarcely more than a nasty little back-alley, lined with a few dingy shop-fronts: strip joints, sex clubs and porn emporia with blanked-out windows. Mistress Mine stood out in stark contrast to the other shops, its depravity not shabby or seedy, but brash and glossy.

She didn't especially want to be seen hovering outside a sex shop, a strip joint or a fetishwear boutique; a nagging anxiety kept telling her it really wasn't safe. She tried walking up and down the street, to give the impression that she was looking in other shops windows, but that hardly helped, since there seemed to be nothing in this dingy little cobbled street that wasn't intimately connected with the sex industry. Marcie began to wish she'd worn something less alluring. The short skirt and sleeveless top she had chosen to please Richard might also please other, less innocent, passers-by.

A vague unease drew her gaze back, time and time again, to the gleaming black Mercedes parked across the end of the street. There were two men inside, anonymous in dark glasses and business suits. Marcie couldn't escape the feeling that they were watching her. Maybe she should leave, after all. She turned round and started walking in the opposite direction, feeling immediately better as she put more distance between herself and the two men. Richard would just have to guess what had happened to her. Too bad. It was his fault for choosing such a bizarre place for a rendezvous.

Her heart sank as she rounded the corner and realised the awful truth: the alleyway ended in a blank wall, the end of a tumbledown terrace of Victorian shops. Damn! There was no way out of the alley, except by walking past the two men in the Mercedes.

She stood for a few moments, just gazing up at the crumbling brick wall which had confounded her. Oh well, she would just have to swallow her pride, turn round and go back the way she'd come.

Footsteps.

Richard? No: two sets of footsteps; the sound of steel-tipped heels striking against the cobbled roadway.

Footsteps behind her, still a little way off, but getting closer. Marcie held her breath, paralysed with sudden fear. Some sixth sense forbade her to turn round, kept her staring forwards like an idiot at the blank wall in front of her.

The heavy tread of two unseen figures. It didn't take a genius to guess who they were. They were right behind her now, perhaps close enough to touch. Two dark shadows loomed above her on the soot-blackened wall.

The voice was harsh but quiet, hardly more than a whisper in her ear. He was so close to her that her lungs filled with the cloying sweetness of his breath.

'You in business, darlin'?'

The words electrified her, brought home to her with dreadful clarity the role she was being asked to play. Of course, she could say no; she could walk away; or run; or scream for help. But who would hear her?

'I don't know what you mean . . .'

The lie was hollow and unconvincing; the tremble in Marcie's voice sounded more like the urgency of desire than the uncertainty of fear.

'Don't play games with me, sweetheart.' There was menace in the voice now; and a hand clamped itself on Marcie's arm, squeezing so tightly that she gasped with the discomfort and tried to wriggle free. But the hand was inexorable and she could not prise the fingers away from her arm. They were making little whitish indentations in the soft tanned flesh; indentations which would later turn to bluish bruises.

'Don't play games. I could break you like a doll if I wanted to.' As though to emphasise his message, the men tightened his grip on her arm. There was a terrible power in that grip, a dreadful truth in his words. 'Your sort are all the same. Think you're so bloody powerful. You're prick-teasers, the lot of you. All you really care about is the cash. But don't you worry, darlin'. We'll pay you well.'

'I'm not – not what you think I am,' Marcie gasped, half-suffocated by the arm round her breasts, pulling her backwards into the man's body.

'Oh, I know exactly what you are.'

She felt herself dragged backwards by an overwhelming strength. She tried to resist, but it was useless. She couldn't even find the will to cry out. There was a curious excitement in her fear.

Where was he taking her? Back down the alleyway. Was he going to make her go into one of those horrible grimy strip joints? Oh God, no;

what would they do to her in there, alone in the deep unfriendly darkness? Where the hell was Richard?

A shop-front loomed in front of her, a riot of glossy black and red paint; the neon sign an insolent, unblinking blue: *Mistress Mine*. They were taking her to the shop. But why? Was this some elaborate joke Richard had organised to teach her a lesson? But it all felt so terrifyingly real.

She felt herself pushed up against the shop window pane, almost as if the man was trying to force her to look into the window, to understand and live what she was seeing.

She had lied to him. She knew only too well what he wanted; and more than that, she knew to her shame that a part of her wanted it, too. Richard had spoken of an adventure. Well, this might not be quite the adventure he had planned, but the adrenalin was pumping through Marcie's veins. These last weeks had changed her. She, who had always loved the sunlight and the warmth, had grown to understand the allure of the darkness, the chill dank world of the night-children.

I should turn round, Marcie told herself. Turn round and confront him. Tell him I won't be a slave to his depraved desires. But she kept on staring into the shop window, as rough hands spoke to her more eloquently than other words. And little by little she yielded, body and mind, to the intoxication of a chance encounter in a sordid backstreet.

The centrepiece of the window display consisted of two models: one a man, dressed as an executioner, masked and with a studded leather belt, and tight pants bulging at the crotch. He was wielding a belt, a double-thonged tawse, which he was about to bring down on the creamy-white buttocks of the girl before him. She was dressed in a black bondage bra, and her wrists were chained behind her back, attached to the spiked dog-collar around her neck. Other than that, she was naked, save for her shiny red thigh-length boots.

She was on her knees, bending forward over an executioner's block, her long, blonde hair tumbling forwards and concealing her face. Her back was arched and her thighs spread, her buttocks parted and, it seemed to Marcie, trembling with eagerness for her tormentor's lash. The scene was pure kitsch, but as Marcie looked on, it became her world, her only existence. Like the naked girl, she too was surrendering to guilty desires.

There was a strange eroticism to this bizzare tableau, and Marcie felt a familiar warmth in her belly as a bold hand massaged her buttocks, exploring their firmness with practised skill. She dared not move. Did she really want to? What if he had a knife? What if he intended to harm her? The street was utterly deserted now, save for the unseen businessman and his companion, parked down the street in the black Mercedes. Unless they were the men with her now. She was utterly alone.

Only the faint hum of distant traffic reminded Marcie that another, saner world existed, beyond this underworld of sex for sale. She could still resist; could still choose liberty and sunshine. Something told her that this man, so bold and so threatening, would not harm her if she rejected him. There was a softness in his touch, a compelling warmth spreading from his eager fingers as they grew bolder still, sliding swiftly downwards, until they met the hem of her skirt and disappeared underneath.

She was pressed up hard against the glass now, more than ever a part of the scene she saw before her. In her mind, she was now the blonde-haired slave, submitting her soft whiteness to the lover's lash, accepting the punishment of tyrannical love with patient resignation. Perhaps even with joy.

The hand explored Marcie's thighs, skirting her stocking-tops and suspenders, and moving on quickly upwards. She realised with horror what discovery her assailant would make next.

'My darling little slut!' hissed a voice in her ear. 'You have prepared the way for me so beautifully!'

Marcie's face reddened with shame, the bare flesh of her naked womanhood damning her to the role she had so valiantly denied. She remembered how she had laughed as she cast aside her panties that morning, and chosen to walk naked beneath her skirt. She had meant it as a way of pleasuring Richard that afternoon, when they got to the hotel.

Despite her fears, she found herself mesmerised by the probing finger, and instinctively slid her legs as far apart as her tight skirt would allow. The unseen demon-lover anticipated her thoughts, and slid the skirt upwards, exposing Marcie's naked flesh. She pressed her face up against the cool, cool glass, behind which the shameless girl was still arching her back in joyous submission.

His other hand was on her breasts now, burrowing up underneath her blouse and pinching her left nipple, so hard that she moaned with discomfort and pleasure. His fingers left off tormenting the amber furrow between her backside, and slid forward, toying with the juices that were by now flowing like a fragrant river from between her love-lips. Unseen, his presence was nothing more than a dark shadow in the shop window, looming up above the scene she was forced to watch. It was like being seduced by some lewd phantom.

There was a sudden movement, and Marcie felt a throbbing hardness against the naked flesh of her backside. She struggled a little, but her protests were insincere, and he knew it. He knew as well as Marcie did that she was desperate for him, longing for him to do with her exactly as he wished, just as the masked executioner was doing with his silent and willing victim.

Prising her apart as though she were some ripe and yielding fruit, Marcie's unseen lover slid his throbbing dick into her hot wetness. Like a sword into a scabbard it slid home, tightly sheathed in warm flesh. Marcie accepted the instrument of martyrdom with silent joy. It was massive, hard and magnificently thick, but she dared not cry out, for fear that someone would overhear and come out of one of the shops to see what was happening. She pressed her hand into her mouth to stifle little cries of pleasure and distress. To her surprise, Marcie found herself growing more and more excited as she stood there, squashed up against the glass with her skirt around her waist, fucking like the shameless little animal she suddenly longed to be. And all along, the blonde girl in the shop window arched her back in the silent, patient anticipation of ecstasy; an ecstasy that would be forever an instant away.

He rode her with a rough urgency which excited her even more. Marcie could feel him growing harder, and knew he would soon come. Would he assert his power over her by leaving her unsatisfied? Slyly, he slipped a finger inside her furrow, feeling for the pulsating centre of her pleasure. But there was no need for him to bring her brutally to her climax. The lightest touch of his fingertips on her outer lips was enough to send the first delicious shivers of her orgasm racing through her body. In the same instant, the unseen lover withdrew from her, and she felt the hot rush of his semen spattering triumphantly all over her tanned buttocks.

Her passion unfettered at last, Marcie lost all control of herself, and as she climaxed shamelessly, she sobbed out her pleasure. The blonde girl seemed to join with her in the consummation of her joy.

When at last she caught her breath and opened her eyes, her unseen lover was gone, and the black Mercedes was reversing away, out of the sidestreet. Marcie was alone outside the shop: to all intents and purposes a little slut with dewdrops of love-juice trickling down her thighs.

She tried desperately to cover herself up, but as she struggled to pull down her skirt the door of Mistress Mine swung open. She looked up in bewilderment and dismay at the leather-clad figure, enigmatic as ever behind the darkened visor.

'Come inside, Marcie.' The biker extended a gloved hand towards her, steel studs gleaming on the knuckles of his gauntlets. 'So far you have done well: but your education is just beginning.'

The hand was stretching out to her, commanding her to follow. She stood there, rooted to the spot. Seeing her hesitation, the biker took a step forward.

'Don't be a fool, Marcie. You've come home at last. Don't let us down now.'

He seemed dazzling, unreal; a creature of glass and shiny metal, coolly intent upon devouring her soul. Deep within her, Marcie's body was crying out: obey! obey! Surrender yourself to this greater will. Lose yourself in this greater purpose.

His leather-gloved fingertip brushed her face, pushing back a tendril of her red hair.

'Omega loves you.'

'No! Keep away from me!'

Suddenly galvanised into defiant life, Marcie lunged forward and pushed the biker out of the way. Caught off balance, he stumbled backwards and clutched at the doorframe.

It gave her just enough time to take to her heels. Taking off her sandals, Marcie sped barefoot down the alleyway towards the sunlight at the end. It was like running down a darkened railway tunnel, hoping and praying that you will not meet a thundering express speeding towards you out of the light.

Run, run, run. She scarcely knew what she was running from, unless it was the inevitability of her damnation.

Down the street. Should she turn left or right? She glanced back over her shoulder, and saw the biker walking towards her, with dreadful but inexorable slowness, as though he knew she could not escape him, and there was no point in hurrying to catch up with her.

She emerged into brilliant sunshine on what was normally a busy side-street, full of colour and life.

She'd be OK there, she was sure she would. There would be lots of people there. All she would need to do was walk up to someone and ask them for help.

Today, for some unaccountable reason, it was virtually deserted. A road works sign gave a clue: traffic had been diverted onto a different route round the one-way system. Marcie panicked. What was she going to do? Already her lungs ached with the effort of running, and fit as she was, she was no fool: she knew she couldn't outrun an athletic young man if he was intent on catching her.

She darted glances around her for a means of escape. Over there – a policewoman! But no: before Marcie could shout, the WPC climbed into a panda car, slammed the door shut and disappeared round the corner into oblivion.

And then she saw it. Parked with the front wheel up on the pavement. A familiar monster in snarling black and scything chrome.

The Harley! The Harley-Davidson.

She stroked the handlebars with trembling fingertips. They were warm from the sun, like the antennae of some strange insect. And as she stared in disbelief, Marcie realised that the keys were dangling from the ignition.

Marcie Isabel Claire MacLean hadn't driven any sort of motorbike since that little moped she'd bought on her sixteenth birthday. That had been light as a pushbike, and hardly more difficult to manoeuvre. She seriously doubted her ability even to get this one off its stand. But this was her one chance of salvation, and she was sure as heck going to take it. She didn't think to question why the biker had left the keys in the ignition, almost as a cruel bait. She glanced behind her, and her heart sank as she saw the biker emerging from the alleyway, remorseless and slow as a glacier.

In the strength of her terror, Marcie seized hold of the bike and rocked it until at last it rolled off the pavement into the road. Clumsily, she kicked away the stand. The bike was incredibly heavy, and sagged dangerously, dragging at her arms. If she were accidentally to tilt it a little too far to one side, it would be over and she with it.

Straddling the bike, she pressed the ignition button and the machine roared into life. Its power was terrifying, bestial in its fury. With a deep breath she depressed the clutch, engaged first gear and opened up the throttle.

The Harley spluttered, juddered and then leapt forward. Marcie hung on for grim death, aiming the bike down the empty street towards life, normality, freedom.

She took the corner slowly, but it felt like the wall of death as she leant into the bend. And then she was out on the main road, surrounded by the hubbub of lunchtime traffic.

Just keep going. Don't think about it. Into third; easy now. That's it! She was getting the hang of it. The power between her thighs was intoxicating; a delirium of pleasure was overtaking her. Mustn't get over-confident. But she was free! She wanted to laugh, cry, open up that throttle as far as it would go and ride, ride, ride.

The bike coughed twice, and the engine died. Marcie grappled with its weight and cursed as it slowed. A security van emerged from nowhere, a huge wall of dark metal looming over her like the shadow of a great black bat. Marcie tried to turn the slow-moving dead weight of the Harley, but it was too late. She was dimly aware of dark figures converging on her, holding her upright, hustling her towards the rear of the van.

As she was pushed into the dark steel cave, a single image filled Marcie's mind. The image of a symbol painted on the side of the van.

A silver Omega on a ground of midnight black.

Chapter Eleven

There was blackness all around. Her eyes were open, yet she could see nothing. But there were voices in the darkness: whispers that filled her head like a flutter of sable-winged butterflies. She had been asleep. Suddenly she remembered: the shop, the motorbike, the inside of the van. It had been warm and soft in there. She had slept.

She tried to sit up, but her head swam and strong hands pressed her back down onto the slick smoothness of satin sheets.

'Where?'

'You are with friends now, Marcie.'

'Friends? I don't understand.'

'You are with Omega.'

There was a pin-prick of pain in her right arm and then consciousness ebbed away again; leaving only the shadows, which gathered about her like dark angels, singing her into eternal sleep.

* * *

This was a new blackness. Not now the natural darkness of an unlit, shuttered room; but an intentional gloom. There was a pressure on her eyelids, as though something was weighing them down. She tried to raise her hand to brush it away, but her hands were held fast: tied with a silken cord, she realised, behind the back of the chair. The air was cool, almost chill, on her bare arms. With a start of fear, she realised that she was naked.

'It is useless to struggle, Marcie. You cannot remove the blindfold, and the ropes about your wrists are securely tied.'

The voice was smooth and sweet, with just a touch of menace.

'Why am I here? What are you doing with me?'

Only echoing silence answered her pleas.

'Why won't you tell me what you want from me? What have I done to deserve this? If it's money you want, I can pay.'

A ripple of laughter ran around the room. So she was not alone with her tormentor.

'You have been chosen, Marcie. Is your memory so short that you have forgotten Omega's commands? You have not always been obedient, Marcie. You have risked Omega's displeasure.'

Anger and fear brought tears to Marcie's eyes, but she would not show her emotions. The moisture soaked silently into the silky fabric.

'And why should I owe obedience to this – Omega?'

'Because Omega loves you, Marcie. Omega's love alone is true.'

'Then it is a strange kind of love. A love that seeks only to humiliate and deprave.'

A different voice now. Bittersweet with authority.

'No, Marcie. A love that seeks only the genesis of true understanding. A love that trains the senses to attain new heights of pleasure, through the joys of obedience and control.'

There was a silence. Marcie thought she could hear the sound of breathing, very close by. But she could be mistaken; the blindfold made her so disorientated, so helpless. Did she recognise the voices? A strange echoing quality distorted them, a though they were speaking to her from within a deep, dark cave. There were hints of recognition, and then nothing; she could not be sure. Did she know anything any more? If the voices belonged to the people she suspected . . . But her suspicions were wilder than the truth could possibly be.

'Are you afraid of the dark, Marcie?'

This third voice was smooth, velvety, sensual. It chilled her and excited her at the same time. She tried to make out where the voice was coming from, but the blindfold excluded even the tiniest glimmer of light, and she felt hopelessly adrift. She tried to move, but the silken cord kept her hands firmly anchored behind the back of the rickety wooden chair.

'Answer me, Marcie.' There was a touch of menace in the honeyed tones.

'I don't know.'

Her mouth was dry and her pulse was starting to race. Why was all this happening to her? Her mind drifted back to those days, only weeks ago, when all had been sunshine and thoughtless, innocent wickedness. Afternoons spent laughing and sighing in the long grass under the apple trees, while Alex knelt between her legs and ran his warm, moist tongue up her inner thighs, tantalising her for an eternity before at last allowing its muscular tip to wriggle delightfully between her plump pussy-lips.

It all seemed so very far away now: some fanciful children's game. Had she really been so innocent in the ways of lust, so naive, so smug and self-assured in a world of cosy liaisons? Now, the only reality was the darkness.

Marcie's heart was thumping in her chest, her nipples stiffening in spite of her fear. In these last few weeks, fear had become her friend; the spice without which sex had become bland and tasteless. There was a faint, guilty throb of pleasure between her thighs. She felt despicable, shameful; and yet it was as though the fear and shame had brought her suddenly to life, making her instantly alert to every sound, every sensation. Her breathing quickened. She wanted to run away, but there was nowhere to run to, no way to get free.

Did she really want to run away?

'Omega has chosen you, Marcie. Why do you seek to resist?'

Silence. And then the same voice again. A strange voice, heavy with sex and yet impersonal, disembodied, inhuman.

'Are you afraid of the dark? You must answer me.'

'I . . . I am afraid.'

'Describe your fear to me. I want to feel it.'

Marcie searched for the words, but found only pictures.

'A filthy alleyway at midnight; mist; a hand on my shoulder. Other hands, pulling at my clothes;

204

tearing them off me and I am trying to scream. There are people nearby, they could help me. But no sound is coming out. Hands; strong, merciless hands. So, so afraid.'

'What else can you see, Marcie? What else can you feel?'

'A hand at the waistband of my panties, pulling them down over my bottom. I . . . I can't see his face, but I can feel his fingers, sliding down my belly and slipping inside my wetness. I fear him, and yet I want him so much! My cunt is so hot and wet.'

She could hardly believe the words coming out of her mouth; and yet the pictures were there in her head, so vivid that for a moment she almost believed that they were real. Perhaps they had drugged her, slipped something into the brandy they had forced between her lips. Why, she could even feel the hands.

Hands. Real hands now, strong and skilful. Fingers sliding over her flesh. For the first time she realised that, quite instinctively, she was sliding her feet apart, inviting the unseen hands to do what they would with her. She felt colour rise to her cheeks as shame overwhelmed her. But shamelessness parted her thighs, opening her flesh to unseen pleasure or pain.

A finger slid up the inside of her thigh, and she gave an involuntary moan of unexpected pleasure as it slipped between her sex-lips and pressed gently on the throbbing heart of her womanhood.

'Omega knows you are a born courtesan, Marcie. You will serve our purposes well. Already you have shown us the depth of your depravity. Now that you are among us, we shall teach you the pleasure of darkness, the darkness of pleasure.'

The blindfold fell from Marcie's eyes, and she blinked in the orange glow from a single candle. She looked down, and saw a masked woman kneeling between her thighs, naked and lascivious. She tried to escape the cruel, unforgiving caresses, but the scarlet fingernails were raking delicious furrows along the insides of her thighs. Revulsion mingled with desire, and in spite of herself Marcie began to moan with helpless pleasure.

The woman's mouth was tormenting her now, beginning with exquisite love-bites at the tips of her full, firm breasts and drawing little glistening trails of saliva down the womanly curve of breast and hip and belly. Marcie strained against the bonds which held her, but there was no escape. She must endure this slow, delicious martyrdom until at last her tormentor granted her the grace of sweet release.

The knowing, wicked tongue teased her outer love-lips for what seemed an eternity, knowing as only a woman does what secret, terrible caresses most delight the flower of womanhood. A sudden movement, a darting of the tongue like a sun-warmed lizard's, and the woman was lapping at Marcie's clitoris.

She was a merciless lover, clearly delighted by her tyranny of pleasure. And she laughed with a husky satisfaction as she felt Marcie's thighs tense in readiness for her orgasm.

Marcie reached her climax with a cry of joyful agony, the cry of the martyr who glimpses Heaven at the moment of physical destruction. And she fell back onto the chair, head slumped forward; her breathing harsh and laboured.

'Look, Marcie. Raise your head. See who is come to welcome you.'

Slowly and painfully, Marcie lifted her head and stared into the darkness beyond the flickering candlelight.

As her eyes became accustomed to the half-light, Marcie slowly saw the place of her imprisonment: it was an old wine-cellar with a vaulted ceiling, presumably beneath a mansion or country house. She realised, or guessed, that it was the house within whose grounds Grünwald & Baker had held their annual dinner dance. She and Alex had had careless, unthinking sex on the dry, warm earth. And all the time, this place had been lurking underground. No lights now. No music. No smiling dancers, whirling and gyrating to the thumping rhythms. Now she was in a place of darkness and cold, as it must have been all those hundreds of years ago when it had been used as a place of torment for the mad wives and errant mistresses of sadistic country squires.

In the shadows lurked darker shadows still. With a shock, Marcie realised that they were the shapes of dozen naked men and women, walking slowly towards her out of the darkness, their erect cocks and stiffening nipples expressing what their masked faces could not.

'Who are you?' cried Marcie, her despair mingling with her helpless desire.

'We are Omega,' whispered voices that filled the air, striking echoes off the bare stone walls.

'What is Omega?'

'Omega is power and pleasure, pain and desire. Omega is obedience and freedom.'

One voice rose above the rest, louder and more harsh. The synthesised, electronic drone of the biker. He stepped out of the shadows, still leather-clad but with his skin-tight leathers unzipped and his hardness burgeoning in the orange candlelight.

'You are Omega, Marcie.'

No!' she screamed, struggling in her bonds. But in her heart she knew it was true. She watched in mingled horror and fascination as hands were raised to faces; as masks were unfastened and cast aside.

'Do you know me now?'

Marcie looked down at the woman still kneeling between her thighs: into the cruel, smiling eyes of Jayne Robertson, her red lips still moist from her heartless seduction.

'And do you know me . . .?'

She looked from one face to another, each new discovery, each new realisation bringing with it a greater horror, a greater understanding.

Stanhope-Miles and his oh-so-prim wife Martha, now naked and unashamed before her. Jon DaSilva and Gary Martin. Half a dozen more from Grünwald & Baker, some of whom she hardly knew. Some that she had mistrusted, knowing that they despised her. Others that she had known and confided in.

And Sonja!

There was poor, timid Sonja, naked and shameless and stretching out her arms to her. Her new job had been no coincidence.

'Omega loves you,' intoned the biker. 'And you must now return that love.'

Raising his hands to his head, he lifted off the helmet and turned to face her.

'In the service of Omega there is only joy, Marcie.'

'Richard!'

He looked at her for a moment, but couldn't meet her astonished gaze. He lowered his head and half turned away. Marcie saw and understood his expression of helplessness, the studded collar round his neck, the proprietorial gleam in the eyes of Martha Stanhope-Miles as she tugged on the chain that ran from the collar.

Now hands were running over her naked flesh, tongues lapping at her nipples, her thighs, her sweet love-lips. Stiff cocks thrust themselves into her hands, her mouth, pressed up against her breasts.

And Marcie surrendered herself to the call of desire: embraced the darkness and welcomed it in with joy.

Marcie lay on her bed, still drowsy from sleep and warm in the afterglow of pleasure. The late afternoon sunshine caressed her nakedness and awoke her to the world of the senses.

As the golden rays touched her flesh, they picked out the glimmer of silver against the tanned flesh of her right breast.

A silver ring, passing through the flesh of her nipple; a ring from which hung a small silver emblem.

The mark of Omega.

Chapter 12

'Well done, Marcie. The deal you have secured with Strasbourg Holdings should ensure a prosperous future for us all at Grünwald & Baker.'

Stanhope-Miles put down the file and folded his hands on his lap.

'Now, there's the little matter of Mr Baxter. I feel it is of paramount importance that we should bring him round to our way of thinking. He has a vital part to play in the future of the organization.'

Marcie smiled.

'I have it in hand. I don't think we shall be disappointed in Mr Baxter.'

Picking up her case, she left the Chairman's office and headed for the lift. Downstairs, in his new uniform, Richard was waiting in her glossy black Mercedes; waiting to carry her wherever she ordered him to go. Wherever she was ordered to go.

* * *

The woman with the red hair and emerald-green eyes sat down at the computer screen and switched on.

PASSWORD?

OMEGA.

WELCOME TO THE NETWORK, MARCIE. MESSAGE TO?

She tapped the keys, a faint smile appearing at the corners of her mouth.

MESSAGE TO GREG BAXTER. ACCESS CODE 34518.

MESSAGE?

DON'T FOOL YOURSELF, GREG. YOUR SECRETS ARE ALSO OURS. WE KNOW EXACTLY WHAT YOU'VE BEEN DOING. OMEGA KNOWS EVERYTHING.

Already published

NO LADY
Saskia Hope

30 year-old Kate dumps her boyfriend, walks out of her job and sets off in search of sexual adventure. Set against the rugged terrain of the Pyrenees, the love-making is as rough as the landscape. Only a sense of danger can satisfy her longing for erotic encounters beyond the boundaries of ordinary experience.

ISBN 0 352 32857 6

BLUE HOTEL
Cherri Pickford

Hotelier Ramon can't understand why best-selling author Floy Pennington has come to stay at his quiet hotel in the rural idyll of the English countryside. Her exhibitionist tendencies are driving him crazy, as are her increasingly wanton encounters with the hotel's other guests.

ISBN 0 352 32858 4

CASSANDRA'S CONFLICT
Fredrica Alleyn

Behind the respectable facade of a house in present-day Hampstead lies a world of decadent indulgence and darkly bizarre eroticism. The sternly attractive Baron and his beautiful but cruel wife are playing games with the young Cassandra, employed as a nanny in their sumptuous household. Games where only the Baron knows the rules, and where there can only be one winner.

ISBN 0 352 32859 2

Forthcoming publications

THE CAPTIVE FLESH
Cleo Cordell

PLEASURE HUNT
Sophie Danson

OUTLANDIA
Georgia Angelis

BLACK ORCHID
Roxanne Carr

BLACK
lace

WE NEED YOUR HELP . . .
to plan the future of women's erotic fiction –

– and no stamp required!

Yours are the only opinions that matter.
Black Lace is a new and exciting venture: the first series
of books devoted to erotic fiction by women for women.
  We're going to do our best to provide the brightest,
best-written, bonk-filled books you can buy. And we'd
like your help in these early stages. Tell us what you
want to read.

THE BLACK LACE QUESTIONNAIRE

SECTION ONE: ABOUT YOU

1.1 Sex (*we presume you are female, but so as not to discriminate*)
     are you?
     Male   ☐   Female   ☐

1.2 Age
     under 21   ☐   21–30   ☐
     31–40   ☐   41–50   ☐
     51–60   ☐   over 60   ☐

1.3 At what age did you leave full-time education?
     still in education   ☐   16 or younger   ☐
     17–19   ☐   20 or older   ☐

1.4 Occupation _____

1.5   Annual household income
      under £10,000   ☐   £10–£20,000   ☐
      £20–£30,000   ☐   £30–£40,000   ☐
      over £40,000   ☐

1.6   We are perfectly happy for you to remain anonymous;
      but if you would like us to send you a free booklist of
      Nexus books for men and Black Lace books for Women,
      please insert your name and address

      _____

      _____

      _____

      _____

SECTION TWO: ABOUT BUYING BLACK LACE BOOKS

2.1   How did you acquire this copy of *Web of Desire*
      I bought it myself   ☐   My partner bought it   ☐
      I borrowed/found it   ☐

2.2   How did you find out about Black Lace books?
      I saw them in a shop   ☐
      I saw them advertised in a magazine   ☐
      I saw the London Underground posters   ☐
      I read about them in _____
      Other _____

2.3   Please tick the following statements you agree with:
      I would be less embarrassed about buying Black
      Lace books if the cover pictures were less explicit   ☐
      I think that in general the pictures on Black
      Lace books are about right   ☐
      I think Black Lace cover pictures should be as
      explicit as possible   ☐

2.4   Would you read a Black Lace book in a public place – on
      a train for instance?
      Yes   ☐   No   ☐

SECTION THREE: ABOUT THIS BLACK LACE BOOK

3.1 Do you think the sex content in this book is:
    Too much   ☐   About right   ☐
    Not enough   ☐

3.2 Do you think the writing style in this book is:
    Too unreal/escapist   ☐   About right   ☐
    Too down to earth   ☐

3.3 Do you think the story in this book is:
    Too complicated   ☐   About right   ☐
    Too boring/simple   ☐

3.4 Do you think the cover of this book is:
    Too explicit   ☐   About right   ☐
    Not explicit enough   ☐

Here's a space for any other comments:

SECTION FOUR: ABOUT OTHER BLACK LACE BOOKS

4.1 How many Black Lace books have you read?   ☐

4.2 If more than one, which one did you prefer?

4.3 Why?

SECTION FIVE: ABOUT YOUR IDEAL EROTIC NOVEL

We want to publish the books you want to read – so this is your chance to tell us exactly what your ideal erotic novel would be like.

5.1   Using a scale of 1 to 5 (1 = no interest at all, 5 = your ideal), please rate the following possible settings for an erotic novel:

Medieval/barbarian/sword 'n' sorcery ☐
Renaissance/Elizabethan/Restoration ☐
Victorian/Edwardian ☐
1920s & 1930s – the Jazz Age ☐
Present day ☐
Future/Science Fiction ☐

5.2   Using the same scale of 1 to 5, please rate the following themes you may find in an erotic novel:

Submissive male/dominant female ☐
Submissive female/dominant male ☐
Lesbianism ☐
Bondage/fetishism ☐
Romantic love ☐
Experimental sex e.g. anal/watersports/sex toys ☐
Gay male sex ☐
Group sex ☐

Using the same scale of 1 to 5, please rate the following styles in which an erotic novel could be written:

Realistic, down to earth, set in real life ☐
Escapist fantasy, but just about believable ☐
Completely unreal, impressionistic, dreamlike ☐

5.3   Would you prefer your ideal erotic novel to be written from the viewpoint of the main male characters or the main female characters?

Male ☐   Female ☐
Both ☐

5.4 What would your ideal Black Lace heroine be like? Tick as many as you like:

Dominant	☐	Glamorous	☐
Extroverted	☐	Contemporary	☐
Independent	☐	Bisexual	☐
Adventurous	☐	Naive	☐
Intellectual	☐	Introverted	☐
Professional	☐	Kinky	☐
Submissive	☐	Anything else?	☐
Ordinary	☐	_____	

5.5 What would your ideal male lead character be like? Again, tick as many as you like:

Rugged	☐		
Athletic	☐	Caring	☐
Sophisticated	☐	Cruel	☐
Retiring	☐	Debonair	☐
Outdoor-type	☐	Naive	☐
Executive-type	☐	Intellectual	☐
Ordinary	☐	Professional	☐
Kinky	☐	Romantic	☐
Hunky	☐		
Sexually dominant	☐	Anything else?	☐
Sexually submissive	☐	_____	

5.6 Is there one particular setting or subject matter that your ideal erotic novel would contain?

_____

SECTION SIX: LAST WORDS

6.1 What do you like best about Black Lace books?

_____

6.2 What do you most dislike about Black Lace books?

_____

6.3 In what way, if any, would you like to change Black Lace covers?

_____

6.4 Here's a space for any other comments!

_____
_____
_____
_____

Thank you for completing this questionnaire. Now tear it out of the book – carefully! – put it in an envelope and send it to:

> **Black Lace**
> **FREEPOST**
> **London**
> **W10 5BR**

No stamp is required!

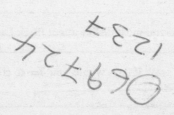